THIS SNAKE IS GOOD

HELEN COPELAND

THIS SNAKE
IS GOOD

Illustrated by Charles W. Walker

THOMAS Y. CROWELL COMPANY

NEW YORK

By the Author

DUNCAN'S WORLD

THIS SNAKE IS GOOD

DESIGNED BY MINA BAYLIS

MANUFACTURED IN THE UNITED STATES OF AMERICA

L. C. CARD 68-17076

1 2 3 4 5 6 7 8 9 10

To Howard, Jamie, and Bill,
who taught me how I ought to feel
about snakes

Contents

THIS SNAKE IS GOOD

"The Boy Went over the Mountain"

THE BUS full of boys turned off the Pennsylvania Turnpike and soon, enveloped in a cloud of dust raised by the bus ahead, was winding through the mountainous country along a gravel road that followed a little river. A waterfall, like glistening aluminum, fell from a rock ledge and dashed into spray. Duncan leaned across the small red-headed boy beside him to get a better look, trying to figure how you'd portage a canoe around that spot. "Hope you don't mind getting squashed," he said, by way of apology to his solemn companion. This boy who hugged a pillow in his arms hadn't uttered a sound on the whole four-hour trip. But now, as Duncan's

1

elbow pressed into the pillow, he let out a short giggle.

Four hours ago the bus was pulling out of the Y.M.C.A. parking lot in Washington, D.C. Everyone was waving good-by to parents and singing "Old MacDonald Had a Farm." Now, singing was breaking out again in the back of the bus. "The bear went over the mountain, the bear went over the mountain, the bear went over the mountain, to see what he could see." The little red-headed boy leaned on his pillow, a slight frown on his face as he watched Duncan, who sang along with the song.

The next verse came out, "The boy went over the mountain . . . to get to Camp Caneechee." And on the next time around, it came out, "The boy went over the mountain to *blow up* Camp Caneechee." Shrieks of laughter burst out and Duncan looked back to see the boys all scuffling and pounding the largest boy, who had apparently started the new version of the song. "Treason! Treason!" someone yelled. The others took it up.

Duncan was envious of all that fun. Eventually he assumed these boys would be friends of his, but they weren't now. None of them even noticed him looking back and singing their songs. What he wished was that some of his own friends from home had been able to come to Camp Caneechee. But this part of Pennsylvania was pretty far from Charlotte,

N.C. For *his* family though, it wasn't a problem. His father had to be in Washington, D.C., anyway on some business connected with youth museums. His father was the director of the Nature Museum in Charlotte.

But also, Duncan had reasons of his own for picking out Camp Caneechee. He had compared all the camp brochures that had been mailed to the Nature Museum, and he found something especially exciting about the layout of Camp Caneechee. Running right through the middle of camp and out to the lake was the Caneechee River fed by springs high up in the mountains. Duncan would be able to explore back for miles beside the creek without danger of getting lost in the forest. In this area thirteen different kinds of snakes could be found, according to the *Field Guide to Reptiles and Amphibians.* Of course, the farther south you got the better it was for snakes, but since this was a virgin forest and had never been burned over by a forest fire, chances were snakes would be plentiful.

Duncan had brought along special equipment. He planned to bring home to the Nature Museum, as a surprise to his father, a fresh supply of snakes, the harmless kinds that they used in the animal-handling classes. Last year Duncan had helped teach that class after school on Wednesdays. In his duffle bag he had packed four extra pillow slips. Those, plus the snake carrying case on the rack overhead, ought to be enough. And getting them home would be no problem; his parents would be picking him up in the car at the end of the four-week period.

The counselor who sat up behind the bus driver came down the aisle in his sport coat and tie, and with his hand on the shoulder of a chubby boy he called Tully, said for the boys to simmer down. "Just ten minutes from camp," he said. Then speaking to the boy who had started the treasonous verse of the song, he said, "Preston, you've sure put out like a weed since last year. What do they feed you at home? Vigoro?"

"Beer and pretzels." Preston grinned around at the other boys, his dark eyes peering through a pine-needle fringe of dark hair. He jiggled up and down on his heels, his hands on his hips.

"We can sing, can't we, Gooch?" the fat boy asked, scratching his round button nose. His nose was peeling. He had obviously been sunburned before the haircut. Somehow the pale band of skin around his short brown silky hair made his head look too small for his body. He kept pulling his sweat shirt down over his new white jeans.

"Sure you can sing, Tully. Just no more wrestling in the aisles. Sit down for about nine more minutes." Gooch went back to the front of the bus, smiling down at Duncan as he passed.

The singing began again. The new version was sung loudly, and on the second round Preston came out with a new chorus: ". . . with sticks of TNT, with sticks of TNT."

"CaNEEchee, CaNEEchee! Rah! Rah! Rah! . . ." Campers at the front of the bus attempted to drown out the song.

Duncan turned around, kneeling in his seat, and added his voice to the racket in the back. ". . . to blow up Camp Caneechee," he yelled.

Suddenly, the boy named Preston turned a fierce pair of eyes in his direction. He spread out his arms in a command for the singing to stop. Everyone hushed and looked at Preston who said, "Hey!" He pointed his finger at Duncan. "That new boy wants to bomb the camp!"

Tully tittered and scratched his nose, but the other boys were strangely silent. Duncan kept the grin on his face. Actually, he was glad to be noticed by an old camper. "Come on, cool it, Preston," someone said.

Preston continued to scowl, his feet in the aisle, his elbows on his knees, his eyes on Duncan. Duncan usually won contests where you had to outstare somebody. He used to do this often with his friends back home. Particularly in crazy positions. They'd be climbing a tree, for instance, he and his friend Louie, and Louie would challenge him to a "stare."

And he'd have to hang there without moving a muscle till Louie began to laugh. So, now, Duncan felt the game going, and keeping the grin, he added the effect of half-closed eyes. But this contest ended quickly. Preston, with a glance to the front of the bus, came swiftly up the aisle and thrust his balled-up fist in front of Duncan's face! "Think you're cool, do you, New Boy?"

Duncan fell back into the small boy beside him, shocked by the sudden end to what he thought was a game, and also at the sight of the biggest wart

he'd ever seen. On the knuckle of the fist a few inches from his face a wart bulged up, so crusty and pitted with dirt it looked like Bald Mountain on a relief map. Behind him, the red-headed boy sucked in his breath and began to whimper on his pillow. The group at the back of the bus, whispering among themselves, came up and surrounded the boy who stood with his fist in Duncan's face. "Come on back, Preston, or Gooch'll get you," a tall skinny boy said. They took hold of him and dragged him back to his seat.

Duncan hadn't moved after the first shrinking away from the fist with the repulsive wart; but his heart drummed angrily. That dumb jerk! That was one guy he could get along without. But Duncan knew what bullies were like; you couldn't ignore 'em and they'd go away. If you acted scared, they'd boss you around like a slave, and if you didn't scare easily, then you'd sure as heck better stay out of their way because then they'd really bug you. Well, he wasn't going very *far* out of his way to avoid Preston. But he sure didn't like the idea of getting socked by that horrible wart. Maybe it was soft inside like a gray bloody wood tick. If it was, Preston would never dare sock anybody with it; it might burst. Preston was probably at least fourteen, which would mean they'd be in different cabins, but what a drag to have a guy like that even at the same camp!

Uncle Murdock

A BLUE and white sign arched over the road: *CAMP CANEECHEE A Summer Home for Boys.* Happy sighs filled the bus, and then bedlam! The aisles were suddenly crammed with boys reaching to the racks for their belongings. Gooch let out a whistle and yelled over the hubbub, "Back to your seats." Duncan was practically in the lap of his small companion, trying to see it all out the window as the bus rolled slowly beside a baseball field. Camp Caneechee! Just like the pictures in the brochure, only here it was real. The woods beyond the tennis courts were dense and dark and cool. Across the road under massive trees with broad, drooping limbs was the solid dark brown lodge. And behind it the glittering lake. Duncan was about to pop. The sun glinted off the brilliant bottoms of aluminum canoes. He saw himself speed out on that pier to the end of it and take off like an arrow in a flat racing dive. The shock would be just cold enough, just right. He'd circle the diving raft and speed back into the shallow water between the two L-shaped piers.

The bus stopped behind two others in front of the lodge. Now the aisle was jammed again with boys and their pillows, jackets, and sporting equipment. Duncan reached up to the rack and brought down a brown canvas case with rigid corners and edges like a lightweight suitcase. It had a large screen window and, on the top, a zipper that went around three sides. A small padlock kept the zipper tab in place.

The little boy touched the window screen with his finger. "What's in here?" He looked up with a frown that pinched his whole face into curious wrinkles.

"Nothing yet," Duncan replied.

"Yes, there is. I see a little box and a book, and something else, something round that's made of steel. Why's it got a window? Is it to put birds in?" This little guy, once he got started, couldn't turn it off. Duncan grinned down at him.

"It's a snake carrying case."

The boy's eyes flapped open wide and the wrinkles all gathered on his forehead. "What?"

"It's for carrying snakes."

The whites of the boy's eyes showed in a full circle around the blue. The freckles came out darker on his pale face, and Duncan read in the puckering of his small features the familiar look of dismay. "Don't worry about it," he sighed and turned toward the aisle. Just once he'd like to meet somebody who didn't react like a moron at the mere mention of snakes. What fantastic rot people would believe about snakes! Like the hoop snake. This kid would probably believe it if you told him there's a real hoop snake that grabs its tail and rolls to attack people. Well, camp ought to get him over such superstitions. All city kids ought to get to camp.

"Watch out for Preston!" Just in time, Duncan ducked away from a tennis racket in a wooden frame that skimmed by his ear. From up near the roof of the bus Preston grinned down, his hair flapping over his eyes. Like a big gorilla he was making his way forward over the tops of the boys in the aisle, hand over hand on the ropes of the baggage rack, the tennis racket dangling from his belt. It whizzed by Duncan and whacked into someone else. "Ow!" the boy cried. "Darn your hide, Preston!"

"That stupid fink, somebody ought to . . ." Preston

was cussed out and called a lot of names, but nobody stopped him. He ducked under Gooch's arm as the bus door swung open, and leaped to the grass with a raucous Tarzan yell.

In three bounds he was up the steps of the lodge. A group gathered around him, all old boys, Duncan guessed from their faded Camp Caneechee T shirts. They laughed and pushed each other around a bit. Then suddenly Preston dashed away and they followed, down the steps and around toward the lake.

The baggage was being unloaded under a huge elm. From one of the low-hanging limbs hung a section of railroad track bent into a half-moon shape; beside it on a rope a heavy hammer slowly twirled. The sound of the one striking the other, Duncan guessed, would be a gong so loud it would reverberate through the woods and out over the lake so that even the fish under water could hear it.

Three blasts on a whistle brought everyone up silent and looking toward the lodge. At the top of the steps stood a tremendous man with a great mane of white hair on his head. Compared with the counselors beside him he was like a giant redwood among ordinary oaks. He was not exactly fat; he was monumental, more than life-size, like the bronze statue of Robert E. Lee on Monument Avenue in Richmond. He was wearing a white camp shirt neatly tucked under a wide beaded Indian belt. His

stomach puffed out in a gentle bulge above it. Duncan had never seen so large a man wearing shorts. In his hand he held a megaphone with a "C" painted on it. He lifted it to his mouth and roared, "Assembly!" His voice resounded like the bong that would come from the hammer hitting the bent piece of track. Then he hung the megaphone on a peg, smiled, and folded his hands across his broad stomach.

Duncan sat on the grass, one hand on the brown zipper case. On the other side of the snake case, not quite touching it, was the little redhead from the bus. A flag flapped in a quick breeze; behind it rose the stone chimney from the roof of the lodge; and even higher, in the background across the lake, the mountains pierced the clouds.

Now it was quiet on the lawn. Even the wind had died down and the flag fell into folds. "I am Uncle Murdock," the big man said in syllables that boomed out from a cave inside of him. Duncan listened attentively, wondering if Uncle Murdock was really as great as he sounded. Uncle Murdock was the camp director, which was a wonderful thing to be. He would rather be Uncle Murdock to this bunch of boys than the first man to set foot on the moon. Duncan grinned and chewed up a dry piece of grass, thinking what a big space suit they'd have to make for Uncle Murdock. "I've known thousands of boys who have run up and down these stairs," he said with a sweep of his arm, "some of them your very own dads."

Heads nodded and boys whispered to each other. The red-haired boy leaned across the snake case and said softly, "My father came here."

"He did?"

The boy moved over closer to the brown zipper bag, smiled at Duncan, and laid his freckled arm on top of the gold padlock.

Uncle Murdock lifted a clip board over his head. "I shall not make a speech. Now is the time to settle in. But, welcome to Camp Caneechee, boys, and especially you new boys. The old boys will help the new to find their way around." He introduced the counselors. He called their names and mentioned the college each one attended. Then he read the boys' names and their cabins.

Duncan was in Don's cabin, Bear, one of six intermediate cabins—Bear, Fox, Mink, Bobcat, Raccoon, and Wolf—for boys twelve and thirteen years old. There were six senior cabins and six junior cabins.

"Carry what you can and the jeep will deliver the rest," Uncle Murdock said with a flourish that meant that the assembly was over.

There was a dive for the luggage that was piled

around the big tree. The little redhead grabbed the handle of a large suitcase and tried to pull it out from under the pile. The bus driver got it loose for him, but when he tried to lift it, leaning over backward as far as he could, both hands on the handle, he couldn't even budge it off the ground. A bulky army pack was also his. He struggled with it, panting and close to tears. His freckled face was now bright pink.

Duncan set his snake bag on top of the little boy's rucksack. "The jeep will take the big one to your cabin. Here, you take this and I'll carry your rucksack. Where's your pillow?" The boy looked around, his finger in his mouth. "Still on the bus maybe?" The red curls bobbed up and down as the boy bounded up the steps of the bus and came back smiling, his pillow in his arms. "I found it. This too." He dropped the pillow in the dust and unzipped a small airlines bag. "Look what I got." He took out some little matchbox series cars and trucks and put them in Duncan's hand.

"They're real neat, but show 'em to me later," Duncan said. He dropped them back in the bag and picked up the pillow. He slapped the dust off. "You take this and this." He handed the boy the pillow and the snake case.

"Light as a feather," the boy said, dangling Duncan's canvas case by one finger. "What are these things in here?" He held it high and looked in the window.

Duncan picked up the rucksack and his own suitcase and began to walk toward the hillside where the cabins were almost hidden among the trees. "Just some things."

"What things? What's in the box? And is that a squirt gun? Why have you got it locked?"

"So people like you can't get into it," Duncan answered. "What cabin are you in?"

"I don't know."

Duncan stopped walking. "Didn't you hear your name called?"

"They didn't call my name."

"You just didn't listen." How had he got himself into this baby-sitting job? Duncan wondered. This kid's too young for camp. "How old are you?" he asked.

"Six and a half."

"I thought you had to be seven."

"I almost am."

"What's your name?"

"Mark Bradley."

"Okay, Mark. You wait here and I'll find out where you're supposed to go."

Uncle Murdock sat at a table in the lodge studying a clip board. A dozen or so boys who apparently hadn't heard their names called hung around the table. A whistle on a braided lariat lay on Uncle Murdock's broad chest. A fringe of white hair curled over the edge of his shirt. "What's the name?" he asked cheerfully, squinting over the top of his lists through his bifocals. His face, a reddish-tan, was finely lined like the faces of old Indians in the *National Geographic*. It was a strong, square face, not rounded like the rest of him. His chin clipped in, in the middle.

"Mark Bradley," Duncan said.

Uncle Murdock's blue eyes twinkled and he took off the spectacles as he reached out for Duncan's hand. "Well, hello there, young man. By golly, it's good to see you. I remember your daddy. He got to be an old hand around here. So you're Mark Bradley, Junior, and you live in Bethesda, Maryland. It's sure good to have another Mark Bradley at Camp Caneechee." Duncan was about to correct that mistake when Uncle Murdock added, "Say you *are* big for your age. Your dad told me you'd pass for seven easy. More like nine, I'd say. Let's see here." He looked down and began to flip through the pages on the clip board.

Duncan's face blushed hot before the curious eyes of the other boys. Nothing he could think of would help. First they thought he was an overgrown seven year old, and now they'd have to find out he was just small for twelve. Standing as tall as possible, he said, "I'm not Mark Bradley. He's over there." He pointed to where Mark sat on the grass peering in the window of the snake case. "He didn't hear his name called. I'm Duncan McKenna from Charlotte, North Carolina, and I'm in Bear Cabin with Don."

Uncle Murdock flashed a reassured smile, nodding. "Well, now, that makes more sense. That name had me fooled. I'm glad to meet you, Duncan. Yes, sir, and it's good to hear a real southern accent up here in these Yankee woods. Not many boys come so far to camp." Uncle Murdock smiled warmly and shook Duncan's hand again, but the damage was already done.

"You're in Bear?" one of the boys asked. "You got to be twelve to be in Bear."

"I *am* twelve." Duncan clamped his teeth firmly together, hoping a fierce look would add inches and weight to his appearance.

Uncle Murdock looked up from his lists. "Mark Bradley is in Beaver, Duncan. You take the path to the left over the bridge. And thanks for helping him out. He's our youngest camper."

Mark looked extra small among the boys on the lawn, but his tight red curls asserted themselves manfully. They glistened like polished copper in the late afternoon sun. "You're in Beaver," Duncan said. Mark hopped up, smiling, the airlines bag hanging over his wrist like a girl's pocketbook. He held out the snake case on one finger.

"What's in here that rattles? Is it a watch on a chain?" He trotted along in his little cowboy boots, hugging his pillow.

"I'll show you some other time, Mark. We don't have time now. I've got to find my cabin after we find yours. Uncle Murdock thought I was you. He must have liked your father the way he squashed my hand."

"My father's great." Mark beamed up at Duncan as they walked toward the bridge.

The Brown Zipper Case

DUNCAN STOPPED on the bridge and looked down at the water churning around the rocks. It was a picture of this bridge in the brochure that had first caught him on the idea of Camp Caneechee. He put down his suitcase and Mark's rucksack and slid down the bank.

The creek that ran through the Nature Museum woods at home was warmer and slower than this one. Water seeped into his tennis shoes as he watched a leaf going round and round in a rock basin; water spilled in and spilled out, creating a small whirlpool. Mark leaned over the bridge and chattered on and on like a little brother. Duncan said, "Uh huh," every now and then, but he wasn't listening. He'd helped his father set up an exhibit in the museum somewhat like this. With the help of a motor hidden under the floor a little stream of water came out of a cave and fell over a ledge of rock into a blue pool. When the museum was closed to visitors, Duncan liked to go under the rope railing and lie on the bedroll beside the flickering artificial campfire and dream about being in the real woods, woods just like these where you could smell the pine needles, where the trees were tall and the leaf mold was thick and springy like a wrestling mat in the gym.

The leaf went around in the whirlpool and Mark was still chattering. A jeep rumbled over the wooden bridge. Duncan had explored every inch of the museum woods; there was nothing new to be found there. And to his great regret it seemed that every year its population of snakes, lizards, and turtles decreased. Here everything was new. Eagerly with his eyes he followed the creek out of sight. He'd find out where it came from and where it went. On camping trips with his father he was always allowed to roam as long as he followed a stream so he couldn't get lost, and as long as he wore his Gokey boots, which were snakeproof.

"Come and open the padlock," Mark called down from the bridge.

Duncan stood up and shook the water from his

hands. He ran up the bank and picked up the suit-case and Mark's rucksack. "Not now."

"But you said you would."

"No, I didn't."

"Yes, you did. I asked 'please' and you said 'uh huh.' That's what you said."

Duncan couldn't help but smile at the persistence of this little freckle-faced kid. "I did, eh?" It was probably true. "Oh, all right." He kneeled on the grass on the creek bank and, with a key from his pocket, opened the small gold padlock. He took out his possessions one by one.

"A magnifying glass! What're you going to do with it?" Mark exclaimed.

"Look at things."

"What's this, a clock?"

"No, a compass. Explorers use 'em."

"Pow, pow!" Mark aimed a plastic squirt gun at a camper crossing the bridge. "I'll load it." He made a rush for the creek, but Duncan caught him by the shoulder and dragged him back.

"No, you don't. There's no time."

"This net's for catching butterflies, isn't it?" Mark said, nodding confidently.

"No. Butterfly nets are lighter. This one's for lizards and small turtles in the water."

"Gosh!" Mark croaked. "I want to see you do it."

"You're not afraid of lizards, then."

Mark shook his head. "I never saw one." He picked up the book, turned it over, and instantly dropped it, as if it had stung him. His eyes flew open wide. He pressed his finger tips to his mouth and stared down at the front cover, a colored picture of a coral snake. *Snakes of North America* was the title of the small hard-cover book.

"Oh, for gosh sakes, what's the matter with you, Mark? It's not going to bite you!" Duncan had seen grown men act just like Mark. He'd have to get over it soon or he'd grow up that way. Duncan pushed Mark's hands away from his face roughly. "Cut it out, Mark. Listen. You shouldn't be scared of snakes. They don't attack people. They only bite if they get stepped on or if you try to grab 'em. And only a few snakes are poisonous anyway. Most of them are very valuable, especially to farmers. They save the farmers millions of dollars a year by eating rats and moles. Rats are dirty and ugly and they sneak in and gnaw holes in the farmer's grain sacks and the grain spills out and gets wasted."

"What do moles do?" Mark asked, big-eyed.

"Dig tunnels in the pasture; cows and horses get their legs broken falling into them. But just one snake around the place will keep away all the rats and moles."

Mark, on hands and knees, looked down at the cover of the book. "But couldn't the farmer have a cat instead?"

Duncan closed the book and put it in the bag. "Some cats are okay at catching rats, but not all. Some just want to lie around and drink milk. But any snake that stays in the barn is going to be catching rats."

Mark nodded and spoke timidly in a whisper. "I just wouldn't like to step on one under the hay, if I was a farmer."

"Nobody would. But snakes don't stay around to get stepped on like cats do. Come on, let's go."

But Mark stayed on his knees looking into the zipper bag. "You wouldn't catch a snake with a net, would you?"

"No, Mark. You don't catch snakes with a net."

"How *do* you catch snakes?" Mark's finger was in his mouth as if he was testing a wiggly tooth.

"I'll tell you some other time."

"Can I look at the book too, some other time?"

"I thought you didn't like snakes."

"I like to look at the pictures though."

"You like ghost stories too, don't you?" Mark nodded and grinned. "Come on, Mark, stand up. Pick up your pillow."

"But I didn't see what's in the little round box." He reached back into the canvas case.

"No you don't." Duncan caught him by the wrist. "It's only a first-aid kit." He took the small red rubber cylinder out of Mark's hands, dropped it in the case and put on the padlock. There was no point in telling Mark exactly what it was, a snake-bite kit.

The path to the left led up to a cluster of log cabins buried in the woods. The names of animals were burned in wood over the porches. Mark clung to Duncan's arm as they read off the names of the cabins: Rabbit, Squirrel, Gopher, Otter, Chipmunk, and Beaver. Little boys in shorts and Camp Canee-

chee T shirts sat on the steps and hung over the railings, gabbing to each other. Mark's hand squeezed
tightly; Duncan understood how nervous he was
about being left with these unknown boys. "I don't
know anybody," he whispered, leaning heavily
against Duncan. His face had the pale, forlorn look
Duncan had seen there on the bus.

"That's okay," he said, and squeezed Mark's hand
against his side. "You will soon. Camp's going to be
fun."

Mark's counselor came down the steps of Beaver
Cabin. Uncle Murdock had introduced him as Perry,
a black-belt judo expert from the University of
Indiana. He was short and dark-haired and built

like Superman, with tremendous shoulders and a small waist. "This must be Mark Bradley," Perry said, resting his hand lightly on Mark's mossy red hair, "I've been looking for you, Mark." He took the rucksack from Duncan and thanked him for bringing it up the hill.

"Where's Bear Cabin?" Duncan asked.

Perry pointed with a straight arm that bulged with muscles. "You go down to the beltline, that little path that takes off to the left. Then take the first left up to intermediate cabins."

At that first left off the beltline, a jeep loaded down with baggage rattled by him up the hill. The tailgate was down and Duncan could easily have hopped on with his two bags but for two boys who took up the whole space by swinging their legs. They didn't even give him a look. For the present he realized he felt the same way Mark did, wishing there was somebody here that he knew.

Don and the Bear
Cabin Boys

THE INTERMEDIATE cabins buzzed with activity. Boys, like bees around a hive, ran in and out the front doors carrying things. Between Fox and Wolf cabins a tether-ball game was going on. On the porches boys rode the railings like horses and kept up a continuous banter of conversation.

Duncan set his things on the bottom step of Bear Cabin and looked to see if his footlocker was on the jeep. It didn't seem to be. The jeep had been emptied and was turning around, its horn tooting for clearance.

The screen door of Bear Cabin opened and a dark-complexioned, well-built boy with thick dark curls came out on the porch—a familiar face. He was one of the boys in the back of the bus who had caught the one named Preston by the belt and pulled him backward up the aisle after the incident with the warty fist. Two others came out and stood beside him on the top step looking down at Duncan. One was the chubby one, Tully. He had changed into a faded T shirt and shorts. He looked sleepy and preoccupied as he pulled his T shirt as far as it would go over his pudgy hips. He looked at Duncan and frowned, his light eyebrows coming together. Then he looked at the jeep as it rumbled down the path. "You've got the wrong cabin," the dark-haired boy said to Duncan. He stood on one leg and tied the lacing of his tennis shoe.

"I'm in Bear Cabin," Duncan said.

"You can't be. You've got to be twelve at least to be in Bear. Don't you, Sid?"

"Yeh." Sid began swinging his lanky arms backward and forward, popping his hands in front and in back. A nervous grin on his face exposed a jagged gap between his two front teeth where one tooth had been cracked. His hair was short, brown, and bristly. He, like Tully, looked toward the disappearing jeep.

Duncan felt that sinking feeling of embarrassment again at being taken for younger than he was. His eighty-five pounds were heavy in his shoes. He

stood as tall as possible, thinking as he stretched his stomach muscles how pointless and stupid it was to try to look bigger than he was. Size wasn't that important. Perry, the judo expert, was probably a featherweight when he was twelve. "I *am* twelve," he said. "Don's my counselor and this is supposed to be my cabin." He picked up his suitcase and the canvas case and prepared to go up the steps.

Tully leaned toward his tall friend with a round, worried face and whispered, *"He's* not going to like it."

The boy in the middle called through the screen door, "Hey, Don, do we have to have a new boy in here?"

"Nobody's going to be new for long, Frank," came a voice through the screen. Then Don appeared at the door, extremely tall, dark-haired and sun-tanned.

"Hi," Don said. "You must be Duncan McKenna." He kept the door open and held out his hand. Duncan came up the steps past the three boys and shook Don's hand. Don was so tall he had to stoop in the doorway. "Pick your bed, Duncan; any one that's empty."

Duncan liked the dry log smell of the cabin. There were four sets of bunk beds and a single bed which obviously belonged to Don, as it was made up with a tight Indian blanket and the shelves above it contained neatly stacked clothes and a shaving kit. Most of the beds were cluttered with comic books, tennis rackets, and baseball equipment, but three were empty—two lowers and an upper. Duncan put his zipper bag on the upper. What luck! It was next to the screen on the end. It would be like sleeping outside. He put his foot on the steel frame and was about to swing up to the bed to test it out when the screen door swung in and there was *Preston,* in *his* cabin. That stupid moose? Duncan had been so excited listening for his own name he hadn't noticed who else was in his cabin. Preston, with a duffle bag balanced on his shoulder, made straight for the bed Duncan had picked. "I get an upper," he bellowed. Then he let out a Tarzan yell, and before Duncan knew what had happened, Preston was sprawled up there, the bedsprings bouncing, his knees bent over the duffle bag, his head on the pillow. He gave Duncan's snake case a kick and it fell off the far side of the bed to the window ledge, where it lodged between the screen and the steel bed frame. Over the edge of the mattress into the aisle, an inch from Duncan's face, flopped Preston's hand, the one with the revolting wart. Duncan started back as if the wart were a black widow spider.

Frank, the boy with the mop of curly dark hair, leaped up to the bed beside Preston's and attempted to imitate the Tarzan yell. "That's Tarzan with a bellyache," laughed a boy helping another with a foot locker. They were the two who had ridden up the hill on the tailgate of the jeep.

"That's my upper," Duncan said. But no one paid any attention with all the laughing over the "sick" Tarzan yell. Angrily, Duncan dropped his suitcase on the bottom bunk. Preston was up there and how could *he* get him off? The worst had happened; he was in Preston's cabin.

"*Was* your upper," Preston crowed, his head lifted off the pillow. "It's mine now. Old boys get first choice, don't they, Frank?"

Frank's curls bobbed up and down. "Yeh, they do."

"Don said I could take my pick," Duncan persisted, knowing even as he glared up at Preston that it was hopeless.

"Don't argue with me, Pretty Boy."

Duncan jerked the canvas case out from between the screen and the bed frame. How much of Preston's lip he could endure, he didn't know. Being told he was "cute" by a silly girl at school had been bad enough, but *this* from Preston made him hot with shame. He clamped his teeth together and decided for the present to just shut up. But he'd be darned if he'd let a stupid show-off ruin camp for him and turn the other boys against him. Pretty boy! A fresh rush of indignation made his face burn. How he'd like to let Preston have it, right on his big front teeth! And he didn't mind if he broke his knuckle doing it, he'd sock that smirk off his ugly mug. . . . It was exhilarating talk going on in his head, but realistically speaking, just how could he come off better than bashed to a pulp in a fight with Preston? The thing was, he had to have friends. A bully doesn't pick on anyone with backers.

Don came in dragging Duncan's heavy foot locker. "All right, all you Bears, bring in your luggage, and let's get these beds made."

Duncan was a terrible bedmaker. He'd rather just crawl into an unmade bed at night than have to struggle over getting out all the dumb lumps. At home he had to make his bed on Saturday and Sunday, but he'd never had to make a bed from scratch. He opened the foot locker and piled his towels on the shelf beside his bed. Then he unfolded a sheet, threw it over the mattress, and tucked it in all around. Not too bad a job.

Preston came down from the top bed, stepping on the lower, leaving the dusty imprint of his tennis shoe on Duncan's clean sheet. His eyes and Duncan's clashed like a pair of swords as they both looked up from the smudge on the sheet. Duncan flicked the dust off with a sharp swipe of the pillow case he held in his hand.

At the foot of Duncan's bed, Preston opened his foot locker. He scooped up his sheets and towels in his arms and straightened up. Several wash cloths fell to the floor at Duncan's feet. Duncan picked them up and put them on the top bed. Preston, his chin clamped down on the pile of towels and sheets in his arms, grinned, half his face pulled up higher than the other. With a quick glance over at Frank and then back to Duncan, he said, "Get a load of New Boy here." In a falsetto voice he added, "Oh, what a good boy are you."

Duncan glared at him. How he'd have loved to topple Preston's whole pile of clean things off the bed! But where would that get him?

Sid, who was making up the lower beside Duncan's attempted to mimic Preston's voice, his cracked tooth gleaming. "Oh, what a *bad* boy are *you*, Preston."

Preston hooked his elbows back over his mattress. "Well, boys, I don't mean to brag . . ." One hand was clamped around the metal bedstead; the wart stood up dark and crusted. ". . . but I'm here to tell you youngsters that crime *does* pay."

"Professor, professor!" Tully raised his hand and snapped his fingers; he leaned on Frank's upper berth. "Professor, do you recommend shoplifting for boys our age?"

"Not for fat boys, my friend, not for fat boys." Sid and Frank chortled like hyenas and pointed at Tully, who grinned good-naturedly. "You going to steal," Preston said, "you got to be built for a fast getaway." He expanded his already broad chest and flexed the muscles of his upper arms.

"I'm not *that* fat," Tully declared. "And I'm going to lose fifteen pounds this month and be the tennis champion, too. I get fifteen dollars from my dad if I lose fifteen pounds."

"Ga, I wish I'd get money for *gaining* weight," Sid said. "I always gain at camp."

When the beds were all made and the foot lockers piled up on the storage rafters, Don said he had something to say and for everyone to sit on his bed and be quiet. He smiled patiently as the boys on the lowers caught at the swinging feet and pushed up the mattresses. Finally everyone gave Don his attention except the two boys at the far end who sat together on the top bunk reading comics.

"Pete, get down to your own bed," Don said, "or are you two Siamese twins?"

They giggled and one of the pair jumped to the floor. "Why can't I stay up there with Joe? I haven't seen him a whole year."

"You've got a whole month now," Don said, smiling at Pete. Don leaned against the door jamb by the swinging door into the john, one foot crossed over the other. His rough black hair almost reached the top of the door. With his arms folded on his chest he spoke in a voice so relaxed you had to sit still to hear him. Camp was important, he said. Personalities were being tested here and it was an ideal environment for a boy to get to know himself, and to improve himself. "In Bear Cabin we are like a family," he said. "We will compete in games as a team with other intermediate cabins and we will be helping each other to perfect our individual skills. But more important than merely winning is playing the game squarely. As you old boys know, at the end of the camp session, success in all camp activities is recognized, but most important is the awarding of the Caneechee 'C.' To earn a 'C' a boy must demonstrate consistently the three traits we at Caneechee believe to be most important for living happy, successful lives in the outside world. These are: honesty, perseverance, and good sportmanship."

Duncan enjoyed watching Don talk. He had gray-blue eyes, neat black eyebrows, and skin that fit tight over his cheek bones. With a beard he'd look like Abraham Lincoln. He looked at Duncan and his smile increased. "We have a new boy in our cabin," he said, "and we all want to make him feel at home. His name is Duncan McKenna, in case you haven't met him yet." The springs overhead began to creak and Preston, making an idiotic face, looked over the edge of the mattress. Duncan felt the eyes of everyone turn to him. Don called out their names and hands were raised so Duncan could know who was who. "Now, let's review a few of the basic camp rules, for Duncan's benefit," Don said. "Explain the buddy system for us, Jeep."

Jeep, a small pink-faced boy with hair as white as his shirt, sat cross-legged on a lower bunk across the aisle from Sid. He began to bounce. "Er, ah, what that is, is you have to have a buddy to swim with, so if one of you gets drowned, the other one can help him."

Hoots of laughter came from Preston, Tully, Sid, and Frank. Joe and Pete seemed not to have heard; they were looking at comics.

"I mean . . . I mean . . ." Jeep blushed a brighter pink.

Don held up his hand for quiet. "Let Jeep say what he means."

Jeep finally got it out. "You have to swim in pairs. When the whistle blows three times, everybody has to find his buddy."

"Good, Jeep. Now tell me what are the big green cans for?"

Everyone answered at once. "Trash." "Candy wrappers." "Bubble gum." "Letters from home," Preston squeaked, "unopened." The bed rocked and there were groans from Sid, Frank, and Tully.

Don just smiled. "No Caneechee camper is a litter bug," he said. "Incidentally, how about writing letters to parents?"

"You have to do it on Sunday," Tully said, rubbing his round peeling nose. His sleepy lashes drooped as he looked around Frank to Preston, as if hoping he had his approval.

"Right." Don put his hand on a red and white box on his top shelf. "This box has Band-aids, antiseptic soap, and merthiolate for small cuts. But all injuries should be reported to Dr. Madison at the infirmary."

"We know all this stuff, Don. Why can't we have free time?" Preston wanted to know.

The rules seemed to be obvious and Duncan was getting bored too. Naturally, you had to be on time to meals and classes. And naturally, no fighting and no noise after lights out. ". . . and of course," Don continued, "no one may leave the camp area."

Duncan's mouth gaped open and he straightened up with a jerk. "Not even in free time?" he blurted out. The springs overhead strained and Preston's puzzled grin appeared. Frank stared down too, and Sid dropped his long jaw in astonishment.

Don nodded. "Because of the very dense forest campers aren't allowed to roam beyond the already cleared land. For obvious reasons."

Duncan stormed inside. *What* obvious reasons? What a miserable rule! "Couldn't you just follow the creek where it's not so dense?" he asked. On the other side of Sid, Duncan caught the eye of Jeep, pink-faced and solemn. He clasped the soles of his tennis shoes together with both hands and looked down at them as if he was embarrassed for Duncan who had made himself the center of attention.

Don shook his head. "I'll talk to you about this later, Duncan, if you'd like. This is a rule we have to keep. Uncle Murdock feels very strongly about this."

Why? What was the matter with Uncle Murdock that he'd run a camp that wouldn't let kids explore in the woods? You couldn't get lost if you followed a creek! He'd followed a hundred creeks! And besides he had a compass. Or you could use the buddy system in case they thought you might be stupid enough to fall in a gopher hole and break your leg. Duncan glared down at the green and black stripes of his Hudson's Bay blanket and mentally split to kindling the wooden arguments anybody could advance against letting boys explore in the woods. And of all places to find such a sissy rule—at a camp! After all the experience he'd had with his father on collecting expeditions all over the country, how in the world could he get lost or hurt in these tame parts? Now, if it was the Grand Canyon where there were hundreds of rattlesnakes and mountain lions lurking around, or even in Yellowstone where bears sometimes attacked people to get at their candy bars, well, that would be understandable. . . . He clamped his hands around his ankles and watched his knuckles turn white as he rehearsed invincible arguments he'd give Don and Uncle Murdock.

Vaguely over the thump, thump, thump of his heart, he heard Don talking about table seating in the dining room, but his whole attention centered on what reasonable words he'd use to explain away *that rule*. Actually, *that rule* might be necessary for some strictly city kids, but *he* should get special permission in this field. He'd begin with the trip to the Everglades. Tell Don how he caught rattlers and milked 'em just like Ross Allen, the famous snake authority. Don might not know about Ross Allen, but the nature counselor surely would. Yes, he'd talk it over with the nature counselor. Maybe . . .

"Fifteen minutes till supper," Don said, looking at his watch. "Anybody have anything else he wants to say?"

Frank raised his hand. "What runs out of a forest fire?"

Don grinned, "I give up."

"Crispy Critters!" Frank yelped with laughter, but the others jeered and Sid kicked up the bed beneath him. "Shut up, you guys; I've got a better one, but I'm only going to tell Preston. The rest of you are too young." He leaned across to Preston's bed and whispered in his ear.

"Quit it, you're spitting in my ear." Preston pushed him away. "Tell me outside."

"Me too, Frank," Sid begged.

"Free time," Don announced.

Preston stumbled into Duncan as he leaped down from the upper bunk. "Get lost, New Boy." Then as he lunged out the door, he yelled, "Me and Frank's got first at the tether ball."

What a heck of a way to begin camp, Duncan thought, rubbing the spot on his arm Preston had scraped with the scaly wart. He had dealt with bullies before, though. He'd get used to Preston. The really bad blow was that no-leaving-camp rule. He might just have to accept it, if Uncle Murdock wouldn't give him special permission. And if so, at least it was a fairly large camp area. No doubt he'd still be able to accomplish his purpose and present his dad with some fine new specimens for the Live Room in the Nature Museum.

Duncan Explodes

"PRESTON'S HARD on the new boys, Duncan, but don't let him get you down," Don said when the screen door had slammed after the last of the boys.

"That's okay," Duncan said. Preston wasn't important. What *was* important was the possibility of some kind of compromise on *that rule*. He'd play it cool, broach the subject casually, not get mad again. As he straightened up the crooked stack of towels on his shelf, he asked, "What kind of snakes have you got around here, Don?"

"Not any. But there's poison ivy. I should have mentioned that in my little speech."

He just doesn't know where to look, Duncan thought, as he unzipped the canvas bag and took

out the book of snakes. There were snakes around
here all right. He began turning pages near the back
of the book. "In this region there are lots of different
kinds," he said. "There's a distribution chart here
someplace."

"Not any more," Don said. "We cleared 'em out
at pre-camp."

"You did what?"

"We got rid of all the snakes, Duncan. You don't
have to worry about snakes. Uncle Murdock sends
the counselors out to kill off the snakes every year
or we'd be overrun with them."

A feeling of lead in his feet held him there staring
at Don, who was stretched out on his bed, his hands
clasped behind his head. Duncan held his breath.
Surely he hadn't understood. He held the book
tightly with both hands. All right. He'd admit certain snakes could be a danger around a camp. Some
kids would be stupid enough . . . "Copperheads and
rattlers?" he asked. But even as he asked it, he knew
that when people went out on a snake-hunting
posse it was *all* snakes that were killed.

"No rattlers, Duncan. None of them rattled. But
some copperheads and water moccasins. The one I
got was about this long." He held his hand level
with his chest.

"What'd it look like?"

"Sort of black with lighter markings, a mean-looking character about as big around as my arm here. I got it with a hoe."

"Copperheads have a brown pattern, not black."

"We don't need to worry about snakes, Duncan. There aren't any more. We made a thorough search. Got them all." Don smiled reassuringly from his horizontal position on the Indian blanket.

"Worry!" Duncan snorted. "Do you think I'm scared of snakes?" Duncan's temper hung by a thread. Now for sure the whole month would be a dud. His hands trembled as he flattened out the book at a colored picture of a northern pine snake. "Was this like the one you killed?"

Don had come out of his slouch; he sat attentively on the bed. "No, mine was more black than white."

Duncan turned the page to a shiny black snake with whitish bands like links in a chain along its body.

"That's him. He looked like that." Don frowned down at the picture.

Duncan closed the book with a slap. "Well, that's the worst kind you could have killed!"

"Worse than a rattler, you think?"

"No! I mean the best. That's the best kind of snake there is! I hadn't even hoped there'd be king snakes this far north. That was the worst thing you could have done, kill a king snake. That's like killing a good watch dog." All his reserves were slipping away; no longer was there any point in playing it cool, he was *not* cool, he was boiling mad. "Why'd you *do* it, Don? Snakes have a right to live!" He spun around, away from Don, and glowered out into the woods. But he couldn't stand still. He strode the length of the cabin hitting each of the bunk bed frames with his open hand. "Boy, does that burn me up!" He turned again to face Don. He felt like a pent-up volcano just beginning to blow.

Don stood with his head thrust forward, his Abraham Lincoln jaw dropped, as Duncan unloaded in loud words just what kind of a dud month this was going to be. Not enough that he'd be spending four weeks with a guy like Preston on his back, not enough that you couldn't even explore in the woods; all that was bad enough, but *now,* to find out that all the snakes, every last one, the very reason he came to this camp in the first place, the *only* reason, were all killed off by a mob of counselors. What was the matter with Uncle Murdock? Was he scared of snakes? Or just stupid? What a lousy camp director! It was sickening, absolutely vomitizing, and he wished he'd stayed home, wished he'd never seen that stupid Caneechee advertisement. The whole dumb camp stank!

His head was throbbing, he was yelling up at Don. In his imagination he was seeing not Don's astonished face, but the bleeding bodies of snakes in a green trash can. Suddenly, he couldn't yell any more, he could hardly whisper. "The only reason I came to camp, Don, the *only* reason, was to get some snakes to bring home. It was supposed to be a surprise for my dad. We need some new snakes at the museum. I brought my Gokey boots . . . and . . ." He looked toward the canvas case lying on his bed. ". . . oh, gee whiz . . ." He sank down on his bed, his chin dropped into his hands, and his elbows gouged into his knees. He sighed. There was nothing more to say. He looked down at his tennis shoes and thought about peeling off the loose rubber around the toes. He had sure blown his stack. Yell at a teacher and you get sent to the principal. Well, let him be sent to Uncle Murdock. He'd just explain that he wanted to go home. Camp was no good for him.

Don stood there a while in his moccasins and socks; then finally he sat down on Sid's bed, hunched forward. His knees stuck out in the aisle. His hands hung from the wrists. It was 5:55. Duncan could hear the watch tick. "Duncan?" Don could do all the talking now, he'd said what he was going to say. And he wasn't going to take any of it back. "Duncan, when's the last time you got this mad?"

Duncan shrugged his shoulders. He actually never had. This was the worst case of sheer, blind prejudice he'd ever run into. To think that all these years at Camp Caneechee they had been senselessly killing off harmless snakes when a little common sense and knowledge would have shown them how wrong they were. But no, people dead set in their ways won't listen. He was beginning to get wound up again. Shut up, he told himself.

"This is very important to you, I can see," Don said. "I'll try to understand. I wish I could give you special permission, but I can't. But one thing I believe, Duncan, and that's that you'll find much to enjoy at camp, in spite of this disappointment. I'll do all I can to make you glad you came. You'll have to meet Holy Toledo, by the way, the nature counselor. He feels the way you do about snakes. But we all have to abide by Uncle Murdock's rules, and he has his reasons."

Don began talking about the waterfront then. Some of the biggest frogs he'd ever seen lived in the cattails. How good a swimmer was Duncan? Don was trying to get him to snap out of it; Duncan would when he was good and ready. He mumbled answers to Don's questions. But there was no point in making things any worse than they were. He listened to Don. After passing the advanced swimming test you could take out a canoe with a buddy and explore around those cattails. There were lizards there too, and on a certain log once Don had seen at least a hundred baby turtles sunning themselves. That he would have to see. The dinner gong ended their somewhat one-sided conversation and Duncan stood up feeling a little better. At least he liked his counselor.

Jeep's Pony

THE SLOW string of bongs melted together in the air and hung for a long echo over the late afternoon lull. A still bright sun struck the peaks of the mountains across the lake, displaying them grandly against a solid blue sky. That bare outcropping was supposed to be the profile of old Chief Eagle Feather, his headdress flowing back and his prominent nose and chin pointing to the setting sun.

To the left of the path down the hill, through the foliage, came the voices of senior campers, the fourteen- and fifteen-year-olds, and to the right, at the beltline, Duncan could see Mark's group of younger boys skipping down hill like frisky rabbits. All three paths converged at the wooden bridge.

Duncan stopped to look down at the water, still weak in the knees from his explosion at Don. Camp might not be too bad. It was a poor substitute, but he could make a collection of lizards to take home instead of snakes. He slid down the bank and laid his hand in the water, comparing its quick coolness with the sluggish warmth of Sugar Creek that ran through the park at home. There were no candy wrappers here, no Popsicle sticks and no old beer cans and broken bottles. Dumb jerks always threw such stuff in the creek at home and the boy scouts were always having to clean it out.

He turned over a mossy rock and a cloud of dirt billowed up and was swept away, leaving exposed a small crayfish. Duncan caught it by the shell over its back. Its tiny pincers waved frantically. He put his finger into its reach and let it grab and hang on. It dangled a few moments and then dropped, to disappear under the ripples. A school of small fish quivered against the current. He picked up another rock, a green one banded with white. His eye followed the stream down around a curve. A clatter of feet overhead on the bridge brought him out of the daydream. He stood up quickly, shaking the water off his hands.

Everyone was standing quietly behind a chair when Duncan entered the dining room. He saw an empty seat and headed for it on quiet tennis shoes.

It seemed that every eye in the room saw him sneaking in late, except for Uncle Murdock who stood, immense, at the head table, his shaggy white head bowed and his eyes closed. Duncan only half made it to the chair when Uncle Murdock's voice broke into the silence like a cannon and stopped Duncan, blushing to the roots of his hair, in the middle of the empty space, several long strides from the chair. "Come, O Lord, and bless this gathering of boys and men. Look upon these fine Caneechee campers and their counselors and incline their imperfect natures to Thy perfect way. Give us full hearts of gratitude for this bounty which Thou dost bestow upon us, Thy servants. Amen."

Now the room was filled with the sound of chairs being scraped back and then hunched up again under the table. Duncan slid into the empty chair. When he looked up, there, across the table, was the beaming face of Mark Bradley. "Hi," Mark said with a shy wave of his fingers. Every little boy at the table looked at him, and then he saw the sign—BEAVERS.

Perry smiled at him. "You looking for Don's table? They're over there."

"Couldn't he stay?" Mark begged.

Duncan's scalp began to prickle. Everyone would think he was really a nut. He felt like a whole parade as he sped up the center aisle to the Bear table and found his place between Jeep and Joe. Preston, who sat at the end of the table opposite Don, smirked, "He got lost all right, but not lost enough." Don said that table assignments changed every week. Only the first night and on Saturday nights did they sit by cabins. On Saturday the theme of the Council Fire program would be discussed at supper. Preston asked why they couldn't do something besides Council Fire on Saturday sometime. "They never vary the routine," he complained. "I've been here five years and they never think up anything different."

"What would you like to do instead?" Don asked

as he served the plates in front of him with hot dogs, beans, and applesauce.

Preston began with how he'd like to go out on the highway and thumb a ride to a place he knew where you could play records and buy blimps.

"What's a blimp?" Jeep's long, thin neck was thrust forward and his short, white hair stood up in stiff, surprised peaks.

"You never heard of a blimp? I suppose you think it's some sort of a firecracker. Naw, you can't buy firecrackers around here. It's like a submarine, if you know what that is. And I don't mean something you get out of a cereal box." Preston leaned on his elbows and grinned crookedly at Jeep. "A submarine, you idiot, is a great big long sandwich and a blimp is not so long and it tastes more like a pizza. If a joint never made 'em before, I tell 'em how and they make 'em up for me special." He glanced briefly at Duncan. I'm not impressed, Duncan said to himself.

It was quiet for only a moment as everyone bit into his hot dog. Then Tully leaned on his chubby arms in front of Frank and asked Don, "Hey, Don, what kind of firecrackers have we got for Fourth of July?"

Don said, "A whole arsenal of stuff." Tully volunteered to help light the fuses.

"Don't be stupid, Tully, they won't let you," Preston said. "The counselors always do it themselves. All you can do is watch."

Don explained that this year they had to be especially careful because of the drought. They hadn't had a decent rain for many months. The rockets would be lit on the diving raft and they would burst into sparks out over the lake. Now everyone began to talk at once.

Jeep leaned in front of Duncan, trying to get Don's attention. "Don, guess what I got for my birthday. Guess what I've got out in my back yard." He had to shout to be heard. Don looked at Jeep. "I've got a pony!" Jeeps eyes glistened. "He's almost as big as a horse, and he's gentle, but he can run fast, and I can lie down while he's grazing and he won't even step on me." Jeep laughed. "His nose is made of rubber and he wobbles it into my ribs to make me move off the grass and it tickles. Gosh, it's so funny . . ." Jeep was laughing, half standing in his seat in his effort to keep Don's attention.

But the distance down the table was too great. Sid, who sat beside Don, was pulling at Don's elbow, showing off what looked like a bee sting on his bony wrist. He made a face as if it itched something awful, pulling his lips back from his cracked front tooth. Pete, on the other side of Don, talked loudly to Joe, reminding him of something only they cared

about. They fell into squeals of laughter. Frank, whose hair bobbed down over his eyebrows, was telling Don that his mother couldn't make him get a haircut. "I told her I wouldn't go to camp if I had to have a haircut. So I won." He crammed a whole half a hot dog in his mouth and tilted back in his chair, his thumbs tucked in his armpits, his elbows flapping into Sid and Tully who sat on either side of him.

"Yay, Frank," Preston cheered, clasping his hands together up over his head. But Tully, who, like Sid, had been almost scalped by a barber, defended his summer haircut, insisting he had demanded a close shave. He blushed hotly as he said it though, and Duncan suspected that Tully had been forced into that haircut, even though he now praised it as a "cool" cut.

Jeep's elbow pushed Duncan's plate aside as he leaned toward Don again. "Do you know what? My pony's got a really unusual marking on him . . ." Jeep's face glowed pink and his eyes sparkled as he looked impatiently at Don, who was not hearing him. He dipped his hot dog without the bun into the catchup, took a bite, and watched his chance to get back Don's eye. Don examined the bee sting on Sid's wrist. At Tully's insistence he said that no, he didn't care if Frank's hair got long enough for braids, or Preston's either. "Who cares what kind of haircuts we've got," Don said, his eyes laughing around the table at everyone. "At this table we're all *Bear* to the scalp anyway."

"Ooooh, noooo." Everyone groaned at Don's pun.

Jeep popped the last of his wiener in his mouth and chewed vigorously. He tried again, this time leaning into Duncan in his effort to attract Don's notice. "Don, do you know what?"

Preston turned on Jeep, his mouth twisted with

ridicule. His eyes rolled upward and he sighed, "Sheeesh, Jeep, will you please shut up about your dumb pony!"

Jeep's face flushed bright red. It glistened with sweat. He drew his white eyebrows together, tightly laced his arms across his narrow chest, and sank back in his chair. He stared at his cold baked beans.

A tray of ice cream in cups was brought to the table. Duncan took two and put one in front of Jeep. "I don't want any," Jeep said between his teeth. And the eyes he turned on Duncan from his small pink face were a smoldering, metallic blue.

Preston's Threat

EVERYONE PLAYED Capture-the-Flag that first night after supper. Campers were divided into two teams; little and big campers together raced around the lawn attempting to steal the towel, which was the flag of the opposing team. It was an exhilarating business and Duncan threw himself into it. Mark Bradley was on Duncan's side. Whenever Duncan came to a halt, here would come Mark, puffing up beside him. It seemed that for Mark, the object of the game was to keep track of Duncan. "You're my buddy, aren't you, Mark," Duncan said, patting the little red head.

A whistle blew and the game stopped. Slowly

everyone moved toward the lodge for an Evening Sing. The air had turned chilly when the sun went down, and the fire at the hearth gave the lodge a cozy feeling. Most of the lamps on the tables were out, so the shadows from the fireplace flickered on the log beams; and the shining faces of the boys who had been racing around on the lawn looked peaceful and content as they sat on the floor facing the fire.

A counselor named Bagby led the singing of camp songs. Then Uncle Murdock took Bagby's place with his back to the stone hearth. His hands were clasped over his stomach. "Today," he said, "as I looked across the lake at old Chief Eagle Feather who gazes ever west into the dying of the day . . ." Goose-flesh crept over Duncan's arms. ". . . I thought of you boys, each one with his own artistic spark for life. We are given a vast canvas. As we walk this earth, out of that spark which glows within, we form designs, as different as sunsets and as similar. Oh, I can just see that big canvas of my life." Uncle Murdock spread his arm and watched it draw a slow arc. "I see some areas where the lines have been jumbled and drawn without harmony. And I see unfinished shapes in dusty browns and grays. We can't erase mistakes, but we *use* them. They become the shade that makes the touch of gold more bright."

Uncle Murdock seemed to expand like a genie out of the flickering shadows of the fire that blazed

behind him and glistened in his silvery hair. The grandeur of his language cast a spell. Duncan sat up tight, absorbed by the sight and the sound of this gigantic man who had killed off the snakes. But Mark was lulled to sleep. He leaned heavily against Duncan, his eyes closed, his small mouth slack.

"And now we'll do the 'Star Counting Song,'" Uncle Murdock said. Softly the old campers began to sing. It was a song about the night and the stars. Duncan sang too on the chorus. "I counted one, I counted two, I counted three . . ." They counted up

to eight, and then sang, "Good night." On the next chorus, Uncle Murdock motioned to Perry. Perry stood up, and all his cabin of little boys scrambled to their feet, including Mark, who grabbed Perry's hand. Now everyone sang the names of the boys as they left the group, single file and on tiptoe. "I counted Baxter, I counted Bill, I counted John, I counted Mark . . ."

By the time they got to Bear Cabin, Duncan knew the ritual. He stood up feeling a mysterious warmth at having his name sung by Don and his cabin mates. Following Pete, he walked quietly through the lodge and up the lighted path to the cabin.

Everything was quiet when lights were out except for the sigh of the wind in the pine trees. Don's bed creaked and in the faint light from the moon, Duncan saw him lean over and slip his feet into his moccasins. "Is anyone awake?" he whispered.

"Yes," Duncan whispered back.

"I'm going to the lodge for a few minutes to see Uncle Murdock about something," he said, and gently let himself out the screen door. His footfalls on the path faded away to silence.

Overhead the mattress sagged and Preston's arm and half his body leaned across the space to Frank's bed. "Hey, Frank," he whispered. Frank mumbled from under the covers. "Come on, Frank, wake up. I've got something to tell you." There was a grunt from Frank. Preston jerked the pillow. "Get your head out so you can hear."

The covers flapped back. "What do you want? I'm sleepy."

"Guess what I've got, Frank."

"Cigarettes."

"Naturally. But what else?"

From his bed, Duncan could see Frank prop himself up on his elbow. The two heads were close together, the whispers too low to hear. "How many you got?" Frank asked.

"Shhhhh! Do you need to broadcast?"

"Broadcast what?" came Tully's sleepy voice from the next upper."

"Go to sleep, Tully."

Mattresses sagged softly and springs creaked as heads were lifted off pillows. "Where's Don?" asked Joe from the farthest upper.

"He's out for a beer and a weed," Preston said. There were snickers in the dark and more shifting in the beds. Duncan lay on his back looking up at Preston, who leaned like a bridge across the aisle to Frank's bed. "All of you shut up and go back to sleep," Preston ordered.

"What're you telling Frank?" Sid wanted to know.

"Nothing."

"What've you got? I heard you say you *had* something."

"Cigarettes."

"Yeh, but you said something else. What'd he tell you, Frank?"

"Nothing. Go to sleep."

"Please tell us, Preston. We're supposed to be a team. What's good news for one is good news for all. That's what Don said."

"How do I know you wouldn't tell?"

Duncan's heart thumped with anticipation. He felt sure that whatever it was, it wasn't good news, but his curiosity had his ears straining so as not to miss the slightest whisper. What was this great secret? It had to be something exciting; Preston wouldn't risk his reputation by making a big thing out of nothing. It had to be even more illegal than smoking cigarettes.

"Please, Preston, we won't tell."

"Come on, Preston, tell us all, it's not fair to just tell Frank."

"Yeh, Preston, that's not fair." Everyone was talking now. The hush swelled with tension.

"Shut up! For cripes' sake," Preston snapped. "Don might be coming back. Joe, you keep a lookout."

Silence. A pine needle brushed against the screen. Duncan lay as still as a stone, his head roused up off the pillow.

"All right, I'll tell you," Preston whispered

hoarsely, "but if anybody squeals, so help me, he'll get it from me." His voice was barely audible, but it seemed to fill the chill air like the sound of a pebble dropped into a well. "I've got *cherry bombs.*"

The beds all creaked as the tense positions shifted. From the bunk beside Duncan, Sid spoke up. "Ga, when you going to shoot 'em off?"

"Fourth of July."

"That's when they'll have the fireworks on the lake," Tully said.

"Exactly," Preston said. "Everybody will be at the dock, so that's why I won't get caught. Nobody will know I'm not there.

"Where'll you do it?"

"Back in the woods."

"Let's all go." It was Tully and Sid together.

"No, just me and Frank."

"That's not fair!" From every bed came a soft protest till the cabin was buzzing. Duncan wanted to go too and said so. Firecrackers were legal in South Carolina and sometimes his dad took him and a bunch of his friends down to the South Carolina side of the Catawba River and they'd blast holes in the river bank and blow up cans. Once, with a few dozen cherry bombs they completely demolished an old tree stump. They'd drive in an ax head, pry the wood apart, and cram in a cherry bomb . . .

"All right, all right, all right, you guys." Preston's voice shut them all up. "Don gets wind of this and the bombs'll be confiscated. I might let all of you go. All except New Boy, of course."

Duncan, who was up on his elbows full of anticipation, lurched over on his back angrily. He glared up at Preston spread across the space between the two beds. "You're just dumb enough to start a forest fire!" he said.

A dead silence exploded in the cabin. Not a bed creaked; no one even breathed. It was as if they had forgotten he was there, and now, with a shock, they discovered him, an enemy in their midst. Duncan stared at the mattress overhead as he waited for an answer, any answer, but no words came, no sound. Then suddenly, a jolt in the bed above and a blinding light struck him in the face. He jerked his head to the side and flung his arm over his eyes. "What did you say, New Boy?"

Preston's flashlight beam bored into him like heat. In a voice as level as he could hold it, he said, "You might start a forest fire; you're dumb enough."

Silence. Why didn't anybody say anything? He felt as if he were at the bottom of a dry well. Then Preston snarled, "Let me tell you one thing, New Boy. You stool pigeon on me and you'll sure get it."

If he'd had one friend in that cabin he'd not have felt so bad as he lay there in the beam of light with his arm pressed hard over his eyes. Every boy in Bear Cabin had dried up like a clam. Were they all mortally afraid of that lunkhead, Preston? What he said was true, too. With the woods so brittle from the drought, they actually *might* start a forest fire. He lay rigid and hot under the heavy blanket and told himself that the time would sure come when he and Preston would have it out. Then, no grisly wart would hold him off like a black widow spider.

Footsteps sounded on the path; Preston's light snapped off. "Whose light was on?" Don asked softly, coming in the door. There was no answer, only the stealthy creak of bedsprings as each boy slowly relaxed into his bed.

The Advanced Swimming Test

THE INTERMEDIATE campers were scheduled to meet at the dock the next morning for swimming classification. Duncan was there in his suit in time to see the younger boys finish their tests. Among the heads bobbing about in the shallow water was the curly red one of Mark Bradley. He struggled dog-paddle fashion to cover the distance of perhaps twenty yards between the two docks. His chin was high in a screwed-up effort to complete the test which some had already finished. Suddenly he caught sight of Duncan and his face relaxed into a big smile. His feet dropped to the sandy bottom and, flapping his arms, he plunged up to the shore, head-ing straight for Duncan. He threw his wet arms around Duncan, chirping like a little bird.

At that moment the other boys from Bear Cabin came out on the pier. Duncan had to squirm around to get out of Mark's clutches. "Is the red-haired kid your brother?" Sid asked.

"No, he just adopted me."

Preston smirked. "He's just your type, Nature Boy. You should go live with him."

That "nature boy" crack, Duncan figured, referred back to Duncan's warning last night that a cherry bomb could start a forest fire. "Your teeth are chattering, Mark. Go wrap up in a towel." Mark let go of Duncan's hand and caught hold of another small boy; he pointed at Duncan. "That's *him,*" he said, breathlessly, walking backward down the dock, waving.

"My hero!" Preston squeaked, suddenly kneeling at Duncan's feet. One hand was pressed over his heart and the other, the one with the grimy wart, he flung out dramatically.

Instinctively, Duncan backed up. He fell into Joe and Pete who came arm in arm up the wooden planks. Pete's frog flippers were knocked out from under his arm and fell off the pier into the shallow water. "Hey, watch where you're going," he complained, leaping down to retrieve them.

"You're too ugly to be a girl, Preston," Frank said,

giving Preston a flick with his towel. Sid and Tully also caught Preston on his knees with a good snap. Some of the other intermediate boys began to join them, but Preston quickly reached his towel down into the water and was up like a fencer to stand them all, popping whoever came near with the wet end of the towel. Again, here was Preston the center of things.

Jeep stood a short distance away frowning into the water. In his oversized royal-blue swimming trunks he looked pale and undernourished.

Gooch, in his snug white trunks, looked especially sun-tanned and strong. Another counselor stood beside him at the end of the pier, studying a clip board. Gooch blew a whistle and motioned with his hands like a choir director for everyone to be seated for roll call. Duncan sat beside Jeep on the edge of the dock, his feet in the water. When the names had been called, Gooch said, "All those who think they can swim from this dock to that one, meet with Bagby on *that* dock for the intermediate test." He pointed with his whistle at Bagby who waved from the far dock. "Any who can't swim at all, meet with Corn Flakes over there at the boat shelter."

There was a little ripple of mirth as the campers grinned around at each other. Gooch threw his arm around the counselor with the clip board and said, "This here is Corn Flakes, boys. He's new to Camp

Caneechee. Uncle Murdock introduced him to you as Cornelius Flakerton. But we call him Corn Flakes."

Corn Flakes shook his head and grinned meekly. "My parents should have known better," he said.

"That's okay. Everybody loves cornflakes," Gooch said.

"Not if they're soggy," Preston piped up.

"Where were we now?" Gooch said. "Yes. Beginners with Corn Flakes at the boat shelter. And whoever wants to try the advanced test around the float and back, stay right here with me. Here comes Jim in a canoe. He'll be helping us. All right, everybody to your places."

Jim was as dark as an Indian and he handled the canoe as if he loved the way it felt to take a long stroke and glide. Duncan watched him circle the float as the first group of six began the advanced swimming test. They took off like racers, but their energy soon gave out and three of them climbed onto the float, which amounted to flunking the test. The other three gasped back to the dock, but only one of them passed the test; the other two stopped swimming and touched bottom. The distance must be father than it looks, Duncan thought, as he watched the boys climb the ladder and flop down on the wooden planks, their ribs heaving up and **down.**

Duncan had been taught his strokes at the Y.M.C.A. in Charlotte. But it was on the canoe trips with his father that he learned how to cover distance by conserving his strength.

His group was whistled into the water and Duncan went into a leisurely trudgen. Ahead, the others were churning up the water with the flutter kick. He opened his mouth to breathe as his arm pulled back. It was good clear water like the lake water they used to drink on the trips with the Naturalist Club. His face rolled under as his left arm reached forward, his hand cupped to pull. The scissors kick gave a strong thrust in rhythm with the reach of his right arm.

He was a good swimmer and he knew it. The trudgen was his favorite stroke. He could speed it up with a crawl kick or slow it down to a side stroke and rest on the glide. He saw Jim in the canoe watching him make his turn around the float. He did a few side strokes and then for variety turned on his stomach for the breast stroke.

Now for the first time he realized that the others were behind him. But someone was coming up rapidly. It was Preston. His dark flap of hair stuck up like a cock's comb when he threw his head back and glared at Duncan. It was an odd expression, as if he was desperately afraid of coming in second. Or was it just this personal feud? Whatever it was, he came at Duncan like a bullet, his hands chopping the water. And Duncan knew that if he didn't move, that warty hand would smash down hard on him. He caught a quick breath and dropped down to the bottom as Preston churned over the top of him. But the flutter kick stopped and one of Preston's feet lashed out and down, catching Duncan under the chin in a swift hard kick. Duncan gasped, his head thrown back. Water flooded into his nose and throat. Coughing and sputtering, he surfaced, a

painful tingling in his nose and the sinuses of his head. He sneezed several times; and when he opened his eyes the canoe was alongside. Jim reached the paddle to him. "You okay?" Duncan nodded. "You've got a beautiful stroke there. Next week you can take the test again and you'll pass it for sure. All you need is a bit more endurance."

Thoroughly frustrated, Duncan lay out on his back, breathing rapidly, rising and falling in the water. So he had flunked the test! He closed his eyes and visualized the next four weeks, a series of incidents like this one between him and Preston. One long series of days, one long crooked competition with Preston. A slow smile came over his face then as he lay out loose in the water. One of these days, Preston was going to lose.

Lydia the Tattooed Lady

AFTER REST period that first day, schedules were filled out in the lodge. And then there was free time. Two boys were playing "Chopsticks" on the piano as Duncan read the announcements on the bulletin board. The results of the swimming tests had been posted. Mark's name was among the beginners. Maybe it didn't matter to Mark to be called a beginner when he almost passed to advance beginner, but for Duncan to see himself down as an intermediate mattered a lot. Junior life saving was going to begin for those advanced swimmers who wanted to try for it. Preston's signature was scrawled there with the other names. In view of that, Duncan was just as glad not to be eligible. He'd have signed up in spite of Preston, but a life-saving course would probably be just the opportunity Preston would welcome to half drown him.

The worst thing about flunking the advanced test was that he'd have to wait a week before he could qualify to take out a canoe with a buddy in free time. Next week, though, he'd be able to explore around the edge of the lake and see what he could find among the cattails. There were sure to be plenty of frogs and turtles. And, he thought hopefully, there might just be a water snake that had escaped the massacre.

But this week he would content himself with exploring the land. He had signed up for crafts, swimming, tennis, and canoeing on Monday, Wednesday, and Friday. On Tuesday, Thursday, and Saturday he would have baseball, sailing, archery, and nature. The nature counselor, Holy Toledo, had posted a notice that survival techniques would be tested in class. They would study the Air Force manual on how to survive in temperate zones and learn Indian recipes for what you could cook that grew in the woods. Evening activities this week would include games, sings, a Walt Disney movie, and the Saturday night Council Fire. It looked like a good enough week ahead.

Now the rest of the afternoon was free for explor-

ing. On the veranda Tully and Frank smashed Ping-
Pong balls back and forth at each other. He'd like to
learn to play Ping-Pong better, but now was not the
time; all three tables were full, and there were boys
lounging on the railings heckling and egging on the
players. "Take it over, Frank, it tipped the net,"
said one of the boys on the railing. He had a bag
of peanuts he was crunching and eating.

"No, it didn't, it was just close."

"I *saw* it. It tipped the net, didn't it, Bates?"

"Don't know. I wasn't watching."

"It was a bad serve, I tell you."

"Heck it was," Frank insisted. "It was good."

"Boy, are you ever a lousy sport." The boy threw
a peanut at Frank. It bounced off his head to the
table.

"Thanks," Frank said. He grabbed the peanut,
cracked it open, and ate it. Then he threw the shucks
at his critic, laughing boisterously.

"Tully, why do you play with that crackpot?"

Now Tully, with his sleepy voice, spoke up. "Go
away, Charley. I thought it was a good serve. I just
couldn't reach it, is all."

"You got to stretch, Porky." Charley laughed
uproariously, his mouth full of peanuts.

Duncan went down the steps and around to the
waterfront. A shout went up every now and then

from a water polo game in progress. The orange ball skipped along the water and sailed through the air. Counselors in dark glasses walked back and forth, supervising the game. There was Jeep climbing up the steps from the water. He hitched up his blue trunks and banged the side of his head with the heel of his hand. He was strikingly pale against Gooch's tan. Gooch was apparently advising him on how to get water out of his ear.

Duncan followed the signs pointing the way to the archery field. The wide road stopped at the infirmary where he had been to be examined along with everybody else after breakfast. Dr. Madison had listened to Duncan's heart with a stethoscope and declared it "sound as a dollar." He weighed out at eighty-five pounds. Dr. Madison took off his big, black-rimmed glasses and let them hang on a black cord. He asked Duncan if he liked pancakes. Duncan said he did. Dr. Madison predicted that he'd gain ten pounds at camp.

Beyond the infirmary the path continued as a pair of tracks with grass between. The branches of trees met overhead. In the warm shade, gnats buzzed in dense patches. Duncan swung his arm through a cloud of them and they scattered. The road ended. The archery field opened up like a pasture where you'd expect to see cows grazing on green grass.

But instead there were three targets with rings of red, blue, black, and white around yellow centers, and the grass was brown.

The door of a little shack was padlocked; apparently bows and arrows were kept here. Duncan jangled the padlock, wishing he could take out a bow and arrow and try his luck. He took a stance, as he had seen it in pictures, pulled back an imaginary string and let fly. The arrow sped straight to the yellow. "Bull's eye!" he said out loud. Then feeling slightly foolish, he broke into a run to the lake that lapped up on one side of the field. Three sailboats leaned into the breeze out there. That was another thing he could do in free time when he had passed the advanced swimming test—sail.

Because of a dense thicket that came down close to the water, there was no shore to walk along. The water level was down a foot below the high-water mark. There ought to be a cloudburst that would end this drought, fill the lake and turn the grass green again. He walked around the field and saw that there was a fence between it and the woods; the low bushes had so crowded into it that the wire and posts were almost out of sight. This was a dead end.

He went back to the infirmary and followed a path behind it that went past a green trash can and joined another well-trodden trail. He ran along this in the soft dust till he came to the Council Ring. Benches made of logs split down the middle formed a large circle. A neat pyramid of wood had been built up within a circle of stones and a pile of split logs was stacked nearby, ready for the first Council Fire. This was something to look forward to. He could imagine the huge bonfire leaping up taller than Uncle Murdock. He picked up a pair of iron fire tongs. He'd like to poke up a spray of sparks with these. Preston ought to throw his cherry bombs in the fire. That would be a good trick he could get away with without risking a fire in the woods.

As he went back down the dusty path, he lifted the lid of the trash can. There was a Band-aid wrapper in it. He put the lid back on and knocked with his knuckles on the side of it. It made a nice hollow drum noise.

Farther on down the trail Duncan came upon two small log shelters. The first one was labeled "Nature." Holy Toledo was in there making a poster. Colored pictures of mushrooms were spread out on the table. "Hi, there," he said. He had a round, smooth, tan face and a puff of silky hair over his forehead. And that was all the hair he had. The top of his head was as bald as a brown egg. He told Duncan his name and said, "Who're you?"

"Duncan McKenna."

"Oh, you're the fellow who likes snakes. Don told me about you."

"That was terrible what you all did at pre-camp," Duncan said.

"Hey, now, I like that southern accent. My mother was a Georgia girl." Then he frowned and nodded. "Yes, I agree. It's bad for snakes around here. Uncle Murdock just doesn't trust any of 'em."

"Do you think they got 'em all?"

"I haven't seen any around. But I'll advise you, Duncan. If you find one, just don't tell anybody." Holy dipped his finger into a glue pot and bent over the poster paper. His bald spot was completely encircled by a light brown fringe of hair. Like a halo, Duncan thought, grinning. So that's where he got his name. He almost mentioned that out loud, but

decided not to. Even though Holy was sure to be a good sport about it, nobody still in college would want to be reminded that he was practically bald. "What are we going to do in the survival course?" he asked.

"Learn how to live in the woods like Indians," he said.

"Good. I'm taking archery too. Maybe we can shoot rabbits with bows and arrows."

"If you get one, we'll cook him," Holy said.

Duncan stayed a while, helping with the posters. Then he chewed the glue off his fingers and went into the Craft Shop next door. The counselor, Jason Cohoon, was trying to divide a block of clay into smaller pieces with a length of wire. It was really a two-man job. When he saw Duncan, he said, "Good. A volunteer." He wrapped a piece of wire around a block of wood and handed it to Duncan. Then with a pair of scissors he cut the wire and fastened it around the scissors. Together they sliced the wire down through the clay, making twelve equal pieces which they put in plastic bags.

According to Jason's watch there was still three quarters of an hour before supper. Behind the Craft Shop the creek meandered along, with convenient stepping stones across it. Duncan looked under each of the flat stones, but found only one small crayfish under one of them. He leaned over and drank some of the water. Cool clean mountain spring water. He would have explored on down the creek, but decided to leave that for another free time. After all, he didn't want to see it all on the first afternoon.

He ran up the steep bank and along the path which Jason told him was the start of the beltline. Soon he came upon a road that curved up the hill. This must be the way to the senior cabins, Jaguar, Panther, Tiger, Leopard, Cheetah, and Lion. At the intersection he recognized Charley and Bates, who had been clowning around at the Ping-Pong table. They tagged each other back and forth.

"Is that the way up to the senior cabins?" Duncan asked.

"Yeh, but you'd better not go up there," Charley sang, a mysterious glint in his eye.

"Why not?"

"Nobody's allowed up there but us seniors," Charley said. His long horse face suddenly looked grim. His voice dropped in artificial distress. He shook his head. "We've got a boa constrictor up there that eats little campers!"

Bates, with his eyes half closed, was snapping his fingers and whistling a popular song. "Aw, come off it, Charley," he burst out, hitting Charley on the shoulder so that he fell off the mound of grass between the jeep tracks. "What do you want to pester little kids for?"

"That's okay," Duncan said. "I like boa constrictors. I've got some at home and I wrap 'em around my neck for the fun of it."

Bates slapped Duncan on the back. "That's telling him, kid."

Charley hooted, shaking his finger at Duncan. "Now I recognize him. I saw this kid at the circus. His mother is the snake lady. She's got tattoos all up and down her and she goes around with this big snake like a scarf . . ." Charley fell to one knee on the grassy rise in the road and tottered there as if he supported the weight of a tremendous snake in both hands and across his shoulders. "Yeh, she's named Lydia." In a creaky soprano he sang, "Lydia, oh, Lydia, Say have you met Lydia, She's Lydia, the taa-aaa-tooed lady. . . . She once swept an admiral clear off his feet, The ships on her hips made his heart skip a beat . . ."

Bates covered his ears. Out of one side of his mouth he said loudly to Duncan, "He's a mental case. I'm his keeper." He took Charley by the wrist and began to drag him up the hill. The song about Lydia persisted till Charley ran out of verses and he and Bates were out of sight.

Beside Bear Cabin was one of the tallest pines that Duncan had ever seen. Its limbs, beginning with the lowest one that slanted over the shingled roof of the cabin, were evenly spaced up the trunk.

It was a perfect climbing tree. From the topmost perch you would be able to see out over everything. He hadn't heard that there was any rule against tree climbing, but there might be one. He'd better not ask; he'd climb the tree and then if he was told not to do it again, at least he'd have had that first look-out over the surrounding land. The problem would be getting up on the roof of the cabin. With a boost he could get to the top of a hot water tank by the bathroom door, and from there to the roof. But if he asked for help, he might be told climbing trees was taboo. He'd figure out another way.

Pete, Joe, and Jeep sat on the top step of the cabin silently reading comic books. Duncan, on the bottom step, began drawing in the dust with a stick, letting the problem of how to get up on the roof simmer in his mind. There were no chairs in the cabin to step on. If he had a rope he could tie one end of it to a tree, throw the coil over the top and shinny up. But there was no rope.

In the fine dust there was emerging from the stick in his hand a picture of a lady with a snake around her neck. She supported the snake's head in one hand and the tail went through her other hand. With a pine needle Duncan sketched in the pattern of the snake's skin, the bathing suit on the lady, and the tattoo on her uplifted arm. With his finger he smoothed out mistakes; he made corrections till the picture was so good he was sorry it would have to be stepped on eventually. He was perfecting the forked tongue when he noticed for the first time that several pairs of feet stood around the picture.

He looked up and Preston looked down, a crooked grin on his face. Tully tugged at the tail of his shirt and said, "Gee, that's pretty good."

"Not bad," said another boy. A real huddle had gathered around Duncan.

"I suppose that's your girl friend," Preston said.

"That's a boa constrictor around her neck," Duncan said, adding to the pattern along the coils.

"That your girl friend in the bikini?"

"No, it's my mother," Duncan said looking up soberly at Preston.

Tully and the other boys cackled with laughter, but Preston only muttered, "Think you're a funny man, do you?"

The crowd around the picture was growing, and Duncan, feeling reckless with success, stood up, brushing the dust off his hands. "Yeh, that's my mom. She's Lydia the tattooed lady."

In the midst of the laughter that followed, Preston let out a yell. "Cripes, that snake bit me!" He hopped around on one foot, holding the other, scattering the crowd and letting out ludicrous agonizing sounds. He hobbled up to the picture. "Take *that* . . . and *that* . . . and *that!*" With the foot he had been holding he attacked the ground, dragging his tennis shoe across the snake's head, obliterating the body, scattering the dust of Lydia.

Duncan turned away from the disgusting sight of Preston clowning around and went up the steps of the cabin. "That guy makes me barf," said a voice behind him. It was Jeep, brilliantly sunburned, his eyes the angry gunmetal blue. "I hadn't even seen it good when he had to go mess it up. Wouldn't a snake that size be too heavy for a lady to carry around? What kind was it?"

"That was supposed to be a boa constrictor, but they don't usually use boas in circuses. They like indigos better."

"Why? Are they smaller?"

"Some are. The main thing is they're tamer. They get to love people. But boas . . . you gotta watch 'em. They get big, and if they're hungry they just might get to constricting on their trainers."

Jeep's mouth dropped open as he backed through the door into the bathroom. "You mean . . . right there in front of everybody, they might . . ." He grabbed his throat with his hands and stuck out his tongue, looking cross-eyed.

Duncan laughed. "He wouldn't care who watched."

"Has it ever happened, that you know of?"

"They feed 'em well in circuses, pigs and things, but in the jungles people have to watch out for the

big ones. Pythons and anacondas will sneak up on a person and before he can even catch his breath that snake'll have a stranglehold on him."

"What a way to go!" Jeep turned on the water. "Say listen, Duncan, somebody said they heard you get mad at Don yesterday and yell your head off at him for killing a copperhead."

"It wasn't a copperhead. It was a king snake, and I'm still mad. Uncle Murdock's a sissy to be so scared of snakes. Don't get me started. Come on, the bell rang."

"Not everybody's a sissy that doesn't like snakes. I know somebody who had a horse that stepped in a snake hole and broke his leg. They had to shoot him. He was a palomino with a white———"

"Why do you say it was a snake hole? Snakes don't even dig holes. Everybody blames things on snakes."

"I never knew anybody that liked snakes."

"Well, now you do," Duncan said. There was no point in even talking about snakes here at camp. These were all city kids who never had a chance to know about snakes, as he did at the Nature Museum. If he had one, they'd find out what fun snakes were, but without any live examples, he'd just be always getting into pointless arguments. He hung his towel on the hook under his toothbrush. "Let's go to supper."

The Snake in the Cove

THE FOLLOWING week Duncan passed the advanced swimming test along with Jeep and a few others. As they walked back to Bear Cabin, Duncan asked Jeep to go out with him in a canoe in free time. Jeep said he didn't want to, he had canoeing third period.

"That doesn't matter, Jeep, you won't have to do anything. You can just sit in the bow and drag your hands in the water. Please, Jeep. I've got to have a buddy. You can lie back and dream about your pony."

"How did you know about my pony?" Jeep asked with a startled smile. White flecks of peeling skin speckled his nose. His hair was almost blindingly white.

"I heard you the first night trying to tell Don."

Jeep sighed. "He's really a great pony, Dunc. Fast and maneuverable like a polo pony and just the right size, just under fourteen hands. Sometimes I sleep all night in his stall."

Don came out on the steps of the cabin. "Better hurry, boys. Check the bulletin board for new table assignments."

Jeep groaned. "Darn it all. I was going to tell you something else at lunch."

"Save it for free time. Meet me at the canoes."

"Okay, I'll go with you."

"I already signed us up," Duncan said as he stepped into the stern of the canoe. The bow rested on the sand. Jeep took off his shoes and tied them to a thwart. Then he picked up the bow paddle and pushed off, settling himself in paddling position, his knees on a foam-rubber cushion.

"You don't have to paddle if you don't want to," Duncan said.

"That's okay. Let's get away from the free swimmers, and then you can do it all. Hey, guess what I'm doing in crafts."

"Modeling clay."

"Yeh, but what?"

"A pony," Duncan guessed.

"Right. I'm doing Wonder. That's his name. Jason says he doesn't know how it's going to bake, but we're going to try. I'll paint him black, with a white face."

"I bet you miss him."

Jeep sighed heavily. "I wish I was home."

"How come you came to camp if you'd rather be home?"

"My mother and dad went to Europe, and they had to have a place to put me. Camp isn't so bad though. It's just *some* people. *Some* people make me so darn mad."

"They do me too," Duncan said, knowing they were both talking about Preston.

They paddled by the float area where some of the senior boys were doing stunts with the canoes. One boy stood on the gunwales and rocked up and down, propelling the canoe forward. Many were practicing for the canoemanship test. They tipped the canoes and then attempted to right them single-handed, without help from the float, by sloshing the water vigorously out of the canoes while treading water.

The lake slid by, glassy smooth. Jeep turned around and laid his paddle across the gunwales. Water dripped from the blade, making circles in the lake. Sitting on the cushion, he leaned back against the forward thwart. "Preston doesn't like ponies," he said. "I think there's something wrong with anybody who doesn't like ponies."

"I do too. But if he had one, he'd probably brag about it. He's just jealous because you've got one and he doesn't. Or maybe he's afraid of horses. Maybe a horse bit him once. Ha ha."

"Preston's not afraid of anything," Jeep said firmly.

Duncan maneuvered the canoe over close to a field of cattails. One of them brushed Jeep's bare foot as it hung over the edge of the canoe. He let out a startled cry and jerked his foot back in.

"Hey, whoa," Duncan said, trying to steady the canoe.

Jeep giggled nervously. "It felt alive."

"Tip over in here and we'll be up to our knees in mud," Duncan said.

Jeep sat quietly now, facing front. Duncan was doing more poling than paddling as the thick mud bottom came up close under the canoe. The paddle was coated with sticky black mud. Behind them trailed a murky wake.

A bullfrog strummed among the reeds, but it was well hidden. "See that log over there," Duncan whispered to Jeep. "Those are turtles."

"Honest?" Jeep whispered back. As the canoe approached, suddenly the surface of the log moved and a dozen or so baby painted turtles splashed into the lake. "I wish we could catch some."

"I've got a net. We can try sometime."

They were out of the reeds now and Duncan was putting his back into a good J stroke, speeding the canoe around the point. On canoe trips with his father, this had always been the greatest joy to Duncan, to round a corner and come upon a sight he'd never seen before. On those trips he had been like Jeep, lounging in the front of the canoe, trailing his hands in the water while his father did most of the work. Then there would be a flock of canoes, five or six, and a party of men and a few boys who shared in the discovery of new territory around a bend. Now, it was only he and Jeep and the fun of it seemed especially personal.

The stroke was a steady rhythm; the land swept by. A clearing appeared at the edge of the lake; three archery targets stood on their spindly legs in the brownish grass like wierdly colored cows from another planet. A new turn appeared ahead. Stroke . . . stroke . . . stroke . . . stroke . . . The slant of the sun put a sparkle on the lake so its blue didn't show. Stroke . . . stroke . . . stroke . . . He had to see around that corner. Except for the splash of the paddle and the croaking of frogs, not a sound could be heard as the canoe cut an arc on the glassy surface of a little cove. Duncan stopped paddling. His eyes followed around the shoreline. Here was where the creek emptied into the lake. He noticed the high-water mark on the bank and the effect of a deluge some years ago. A big oak had fallen from the bank, tearing out a chunk of dirt. The tree lay out in the water, its limbs bare, its roots reaching up, gnarled and stiff. Weeds grew down to the water; lily pads and cattails crowded around the shore, a perfect breeding place for frogs, turtles, and salamanders.

A winding ripple came out of the weeds across

the bright mirror. Duncan's heart did a flip as he leaned on his paddle, holding his breath. "There's a snake, Jeep," he whispered. The snake's head wavered above the water, trailing a leisurely wake of ripples.

Jeep seemed to freeze, gripping the gunwales. "Where?"

"There."

"It's only a stick."

"No, it's a snake."

"Let's get out of here." Jeep reached for his paddle.

"No, I want to see him."

"Let's go, it's already late."

"Please, Jeep. I want to see what kind he is." With a quiet feather stroke Duncan guided the canoe forward.

Jeep pushed his paddle down to stop the motion. It stuck in the bottom. "Don't let's get any closer, Duncan. It might be a moccasin. Gooch said they killed some at pre-camp. Please, Duncan." He jerked the paddle free, bringing up a glob of black sticky mud.

"There aren't any moccasins up here, Jeep. He won't hurt us."

"How do you know he won't?"

"Snakes don't attack people."

"Sure they do. I heard of somebody that got bit swimming."

"Sure, if they bumped into him and scared him to death." Duncan strained to see where the snake had gone in the branches that tangled up from the fallen tree.

In the distance the deep-toned knell of the gong spread out over the silent lake. "See! I told you it was late!" Jeep paddled backward frantically as the strikes blended together and died away.

Paddling in rhythm, a racing stroke, they cut through the water, around the curved shoreline, back to camp. When the canoe was inverted over a rack in the shelter, Duncan said, "Jeep, please don't tell anybody about the snake. They'd only want to come and kill it without even knowing what kind it is."

"Okay," Jeep said. "I think it was just a stick anyway."

Survival Stew

DUNCAN, IN HIS half-awake mind, saw the snake weaving among the cattails in the cove. What kind was it? It had been impossible to tell how long it was, or how thick, from the size of its head. Possibly a banded water snake, but he hoped not. He'd been bitten several times by bad-natured water snakes. They were hard to tame. He hoped it was a king snake. A king snake was practically tame when you caught it. But it was probably one of these: milk, ringneck, queen, garter, ribbon, black, black rat, green, or hognose. He grinned as he lay in his warm bed thinking about his former pet, Samson, a hognose snake. What a bluff he was! Before he was tamed, he would try to terrify people by swelling his head up and hissing. He'd make little faky pokes at your hand; but when you didn't scare off, he'd pretend to have convulsions and then flop over on his back with his tongue actually hanging out. Poor Samson. The postman said he was a "spreading adder" and killed him.

Maybe this one in the cove would be a new Samson. By the time the bugler blew reveille, Duncan had a plan in his mind for finding the most direct way to the cove on foot. He'd tell only Jeep, of course, for the sake of the snake. After last period class he'd climb the tall pine tree and take a compass reading on the cove. He'd prop a log against the hot water tank to give him footing up to the cabin roof.

"Up and at 'em," Don said as he went through the door to the bathroom. He reappeared in a few minutes with shaving lather on his face, whistling another reveille. One by one he shook the bunk beds. The sight of Don's red lips whistling through the mounds of shaving soap got everybody to stirring in his bed. "We have to cancel baseball practice after supper tonight, boys," he said. Good, Duncan thought.

"Why?" Preston wanted to know. Preston had been elected captain of their team and he had insisted on extra practices. They met regularly on Tuesday, Thursday, and Saturday first period, but

Preston had had them also practicing every free time he could work in last week. The more Preston forced him into playing baseball (and he was always a fielder) the more he began to despise those practices. Duncan had finally figured out why the antagonism between him and Preston didn't ease off. Preston thought of himself as the natural boss of everyone his age or younger. But Duncan didn't acknowledge this, and Preston knew it. Every time they met, eye to eye, Duncan felt a flip in his stomach; he would be instantly on guard and quick as a lizard to stay out of Preston's way. He never tripped over the foot Preston stuck out in the aisle or sat in "the chair that wasn't there." During a scramble in Capture-the-Flag he stayed clear of the hand with the wart. And, although he often played water polo, not since the first swimming test had he had to come up snorting and half drowned from a "chance" collision in the water. It wasn't that Preston hadn't tried. Duncan stayed alert. It was a game he almost enjoyed. He had no desire any more for Preston to like him. He could never win his approval and he was used to him as he was, a stubborn bully. The whole thing was even funny. He and Preston were like two dogs that never would get along. One was a big mean German shepherd and the other was a wiry terrier. Every time they saw each other, the hair on their backs would bristle and they'd circle around, stiff-legged, growling in their throats. But then they'd just lift their legs on a tree, scratch up the grass a bit, and stalk off in opposite directions. Duncan once laughed in Preston's face, thinking about those dogs, and Preston didn't like that at all.

Duncan pushed back the covers and ducked under the feet that hung down from the upper bunk. He peeled off his pajamas and put on his clothes at the foot of the bed. It wouldn't be in a fair competition that Preston would ever get the best of him, but in some sudden sneaky stroke. And Duncan meant never to drop his guard.

"Why, Don? Why can't we practice after supper?" Preston wanted to know.

"Tryouts for the play."

"Blast that play. Does everybody have to be in it?"

"Yes."

"Why?"

Don explained, as Uncle Murdock had at the Council Fire, that the play was to be given for parents on the last Sunday. "Parents like to see their kids in things," Don said.

"But if we're going to win that intermediate tournament we need practice!" Preston in his rumpled pajamas, his hair like a pile of matted pine needles, followed Don into the bathroom and kept arguing while Don finished shaving. "How about after fourth period? Could we do it then, Don?" Yeh, sure, Duncan said to himself, trust Preston to pick the very time he had in mind for climbing the tree. But as he thought about it he saw an advantage in that suggestion. With everyone at practice he'd be more likely to get up the tree without attracting attention. So, along with the others, he voted for a practice after fourth period. Getting that compass reading wasn't necessary, he knew, but a straight route *would* be quicker, and he liked the idea of using the compass.

After breakfast he went around to the back of the lodge where the firewood was stacked. A fence lizard that almost matched the bark he sat on fixed his black serious expression on Duncan, did a few push-ups, and then scuttled in between the logs. Duncan picked out a length of split oak with lichen jutting out from its bark like a stiff toadstool. If any curious person wanted to know why he carried a log up the hill, he could point to the lichen and say it was a nature exhibit.

A jeep full of younger campers pulled up in the parking lot as Duncan lay the wood across his shoulder. Mark Bradley squealed as he always did when he saw Duncan; he crawled over the tailgate and ran up to him. Duncan dropped the log as he struggled to get free of Mark's embrace. "You're a doggone little leech," he said.

"Come with us, Duncan. He *can,* can't he, Perry?"

"Sure, if he wants to."

"I can't. Where're you going?"

"The archery field. We've gotta take firewood for the picnic."

"I can't come. I've got baseball first period." He picked up the log again.

"What you gonna do with that wood?" Mark asked.

"Nature study. I can put it in a terrarium for lizards to crawl on." That's what he'd do with it, he thought as he ran across the bridge and up the hill. He'd take it home to the museum for a display. It was an especially good-looking piece of lichen, like a big stale half pancake. He put it behind the bushes by the tank, got his baseball mitt, and set out for his first period class.

His fourth period class at four o'clock was nature. This was the beginning of the second week in the survival course. The group had diminished down to Duncan and four seniors, Charley, Bates, Danny, and Bill. Last Saturday during class Duncan had made a small animal "twitch-up" snare out behind the senior cabins. To his great surprise, on Sunday when he checked the trap he found that he had caught a rabbit. It dangled by the neck in a noose at the end of a springy sapling he had bent over and tied down with a delicate trigger attachment. Holy was as astonished as Duncan. "We'll have Survival Stew!" he announced.

Now, here was the rabbit on the table in the Nature Hut, skinned and cold from the refrigerator. "First, Duncan and I eviscerated him," Holy told the others. "No matter how hungry you are, don't eat the entrails. If you're in bad shape you can drink some of the blood, but don't ever overdo on any unusual foods."

"Don't worry about that," Charley said, his hand on his stomach, a queasy look on his usually grinning face. "You want we should upchuck, Holy?"

"You've got to be tough to survive."

"I'll be a vegetarian."

"It says here in the manual that you're not supposed to eat toads," Bates said, poring over the book on Holy Toledo's desk.

"Not even one?" Charley asked, a clownish glitter in his eye.

"Not even one."

"Aw, gee whiz, I was looking forward to a little nibble of toad."

Danny, a boy from Jaguar Cabin, brought out of the refrigerator several plastic bags of survival foods that had been collected in the woods. He spread them out on the table. Everyone stood around arguing about what should go into the pot with the rabbit. "All this junk'll ruin it," Charley said, waving his hand over the table covered with roots, stems, leaves, nuts and fungi.

"I thought you were going to be a vegetarian," Danny said, pushing his glasses up on his nose.

"Mostly I am. I'm for baking the acorns, not putting them in the stew."

"They should be boiled up first, Charley, then baked," Holy said. "Boiling takes the tannin out if you add ashes from the fire."

"Let's do that," Bill suggested. "We can get 'em soft and squash 'em up and put butter on 'em."

Charley hooted. "Where you going to get butter when you've crashed in a forest and you're out of rations? Let me take care of the acorns, Holy. I'll boil 'em like you said, with ashes, and then bake 'em underground with hot rocks."

"Okay, get started," Holy said. Charley went out with a pot to get water from the stream.

Behind the Nature Hut between two parallel rocks a pot of water was already boiling. Duncan dropped in the rabbit, cut up in several pieces. In another pot, Bates put the decapped and peeled acorns. He sprinkled in some of the wood ashes and stirred it around with a charred stick.

Back in the hut the argument was continuing.

"What do *you* think ought to go into the stew?" Bill asked Holy. He sniffed at a cattail peeled down to its center core. "Would this junk ruin it?"

"Some of it would, they'd make it bitter. Those fiddleheads . . ."

"But we've got to survive, Holy," Bates insisted. "It says here on page forty-one, 'Learn to overcome your prejudices. Foods that may not look good to eat are often part of the natives' regular diet.' If they can eat it, we can eat it."

"What natives?" Duncan asked, breaking a puffball apart with his thumbnail.

"The Pennsylvania primitives," Bates replied. "You can bet those Pennsylvania Dutch settlers tried

out all this stuff, and they didn't have any butter to put on it either."

"I bet they did," Duncan said. "The Dutch always had Holstein cows, and they probably brought some with them to America."

"Those 'Dutch' were really Germans," Bill said.

"That's beside the point. We're not trying to survive in those days," Bates insisted. "It's like there's a war on and we've got to hide in the hills here and get along on just bark and nuts and green stuff till peace is declared. You're not supposed to be so darn fussy about the taste."

"Let's put in Bates's bird egg," Bill suggested, laughing.

Duncan pretended to be all for that idea. "It might smell awful, but it's probably high in food value."

Danny sniffed a mushroom. "Like the manual says, Bates, you shouldn't be prejudiced against stinky foods."

"That doesn't include eating rotten eggs, though," Holy said. He took a testing bite of a water-lily rootstalk. "Tough, but not bad. Let's put one of these in. But not these fern fiddleheads. They're really bitter. If you do 'em right, though, they taste a bit like cabbage. These little fine hairs are the bitter part. You have to get those off and then boil them about ten minutes, dump that water out, and boil 'em again in fresh water about thirty minutes. Somebody can take these to the stream and rub off the hairs against a rock."

"Me," Bill volunteered. He put the curled fronds of fern in a plastic bag and went out the door.

Bates was still engrossed in the Air Force survival manual. "It says here that anything that creeps, crawls, swims, or flies is a possible source of food. And that includes grasshoppers, hairless caterpillars, wood-boring beetle larvae and pupae, ant eggs and termites. Yukkk! I vote for none of those things in the stew."

"But, Bates, we're trying to *survive*," Duncan teased. "Those things are high in fat; I read it right there." He tapped his finger on the page. "You going to chicken out on grasshoppers when it was you insisted we ought to forget the taste and have all this leafy junk messing up our good rabbit stew?"

Bates gave Duncan a long frown, then his face lit up like a light bulb. "I got it, Duncan. Let's compromise. We can put in a few grasshoppers if you'll also add that fat lizard you caught. Their hindquarters are supposed to be extremely protein-rich."

Duncan shook his head. "Can't. I already named him."

"What'd you name him?"

"Murdock."

"Whoops. Yeh, we wouldn't want to cook *him*."

A Compass Reading on the Cove

W HEN THE class was over, everyone had sampled the rabbit stew. No one had been very hungry so there was plenty left over for Uncle Murdock to test. The old campers said he always had samples brought to the dining room of what he called the "Holy messes" concocted in the survival class.

By the time Duncan got to the cabin only Joe and Pete were there. "Hurry up, Duncan, or Preston'll get you," Joe called over his shoulder as he raced down the steps with his catcher's mitt. Duncan zipped open his canvas case and got out the compass. With the help of the log leaning against the water tank, he was soon on the roof of the cabin.

He leaped out to the lowest branch of the tree and began the climb from limb to limb till he was up where the wind blew and the pine cones were green and tight and close enough to reach. His hands were black and sticky with pitch.

Many times he had climbed to the tops of trees in the Nature Museum woods at home, but those trees were babies compared to this granddaddy pine. Now the trunk was small enough for him to grab like a limb in his hand. Inch by inch he went up the last little distance almost to the top of the tree. The cool wind flipped under his shirt; there were itchy beads of perspiration on his forehead. He wiped them off on his forearm. For several seconds he studied the scaly bark under his thumbs, getting used to the roller coaster feeling in his stomach. Then cautiously he looked out at the world. He sucked in his breath and again his stomach lurched as it does when you reach the top on a roller coaster ride and you think you're going to just sail out into space. Then he caught sight of the flag sailing out gallantly over the lodge. A toy flag over a Lincoln Log house. It was a stabilizing sight. Behind it was the brilliant blue lake. The sun was to the left of him. That would be west. The trees hid the cove, but he took a compass reading on a spot just around the bend after the archery field. He lined the needle up at north and saw that the cove

was almost exactly west-northwest from that spot.

The Bobcats were up at bat when Duncan ran into his outfielder's position. "Where the devil were you?" Preston demanded from the pitcher's mound.

"Nature."

"Come on, Preston, heave it," the boy at bat yelled.

Preston wound up and sent the ball fast and straight over the plate. The boy struck out. With a satisfied grin, Preston sauntered back toward Duncan. "Where were you?" he growled.

"I already told you," Duncan answered, his eyes meeting Preston's as he chewed some pitch off his thumb.

Stiff-legged, Preston rocked up and down on the balls of his feet, his hands on his hips, a smirk twisting his face. "You've got pine tree sap all over you," he said.

"So?" Duncan said. "It tastes good." The tighter Preston became, the more relaxed and impudent Duncan felt like being.

Preston's eyes slitted down to narrow sparks. "Don wouldn't like his pet to be climbing trees," he hissed. Turning on his heel, he stalked back to the mound, caught the ball sent to him by the first baseman, and furiously sent it flying toward the catcher.

"Ball one!" the umpire bawled.

"What you mean, 'Ball'?" Preston roared.

"I mean 'Ball'!" the umpire said.

Preston wiped his hands on his pants, wound up, and pitched. A fly popped up. Duncan set out for it, realizing as he ran that he had forgotten his mitt. The ball was high and it dropped straight like a stone. He'd have let it alone except that Preston's eyes were on him and Preston hoped he'd blow it. He *had* to get under that ball and make the third out. Everyone cheered when he caught it, but the catch was like an electric shock that sparked up and down his whole arm. His hand continued to throb so that he could hardly hold the bat when it was his time to be up. He struck out and Preston jeered lustily.

By suppertime his hand was swollen and streaked black and blue. "You're some baseball nut," Dr. Madison said when he examined it after supper. "No broken bones, but you'll have a sore hand for a few days."

The next day after fourth period Duncan set out from the cabin, his compass in one hand and a candy bar in the other. His catching hand was still swollen, but it didn't hurt much. No one saw him disappear into the thicket of broad-leaved rhododendrons. Following a course west-northwest he pushed his way through the dense foliage, breaking spider webs and ducking under vines and branches. He could hear the voices of the boys at the senior cabins and the slap of the big rubber tether ball being batted around. He passed behind the survival camp they'd set up last week and the twitch-up snare that had caught the rabbit. He hadn't gone far when he came to the creek, and he knew he was aimed right. The creek came out at the cove. He finished the candy bar and stuffed the paper in his pocket. Then he crossed the creek and walked in his wet tennis shoes along beside it, stepping high over brambles and around patches of poison ivy. A bright open spot appeared on the right. The Council Ring. Good. Next time he would go there first. It would be quicker than fighting his way through the underbrush.

Now through the trees he could see the lake and the little cove basking in the sun. Squirrels objected to his presence. They screeched at him, hanging down the trunks of trees by their back feet, their tails snapping. A wind that chopped up the blue-green lake didn't fluster the face of the cove at all. Its mirror continued to reflect the tall cattails. Out there somewhere a frog strummed; Duncan spotted it, hunched down among the shore grasses. Another rested its chin on a water plant; its long hind legs and the little front legs with the fingers spread out hung limp. But there was a slight rise and fall of its round fat body as it breathed. Its eyes perched like two green peas on its head.

Duncan sat down on the bank above the dead tree that reached its gaunt limbs out into the cove. He would wait and watch quietly till the sun seemed to be nearing its six o'clock slant. Then he would dash back before the supper gong gonged. If he was lucky, he'd see the snake.

The Fourth of July

DUNCAN STOOD at attention between Jeep and Sid at the Fourth of July flag-raising ceremony. The flag rose in jerks to the top of the pole where the wind caught it and sent it flapping. Jeep leaned over and whispered, "Do you think Preston's really got some cherry bombs?"

Duncan frowned as he pledged allegiance to the flag of the United States of America, and to the republic for which it stands, one nation, under God, indivisible, with liberty and justice for all. There'd been no mention of the cherry bombs since that first night in bed, twelve days ago, when Duncan had said Preston was dumb enough to start a forest fire.

Since then that danger had increased. It had rained only once, briefly, not enough even to wash the dust off the leaves. And there'd been some talk of fires "in the drought-stricken area" on TV in the lodge. Uncle Murdock, in his frequent after-dinner talks, often mentioned "the devastation of our woodlands through carelessness." Duncan thought possibly he was aiming his warning at Preston and the three or four others from the senior cabins who had brought cigarettes to camp and smoked them secretly. But cherry bombs now would be much more of a risk, and Preston might be dumb enough to chance it.

As he sang "America the Beautiful," Duncan decided to keep an eye on Preston. If Preston stuck to his agreement to include the whole cabin except him, Jeep would be in on it. But since nothing had been mentioned to Jeep, it seemed likely that Preston had either gone back to his first plan of just including Frank or he'd forgotten the whole thing. The ranks broke and everyone went up the steps to breakfast. "We'd better watch him and Frank," Duncan told Jeep as they walked through the lodge. "We can tell if they've got something planned."

"Also, we could search his stuff and steal 'em," Jeep suggested. Then he gulped and grinned. "No, we better not do that. He'd know you did it, and you'd get clobbered." They went to their separate tables in the dining room.

After breakfast Duncan came upon Frank and Preston at the bridge. They fell silent as he came within hearing and said nothing till he was past. Preston didn't even look at him. He seemed to be studying the wart on his knuckle. It would have been more normal for Preston to put out his foot to the railing, blocking Duncan's path, saying, "Where you going, Shrimp?" And Duncan would have answered back, "None of your business, Fatso," and leaped off the bridge and over the creek. Actually, it was stupid to call Preston "fatso." He was big, but he wasn't fat. More like solid muscle, one of the best all-around athletes in camp. And last night, in a competition including all the seniors, he had come in third in the canoe races. It really was mighty unusual for Preston just to let Duncan walk by in silence without even any growling and bristling hair.

After first period crafts, Duncan was standing in line at the camp store when he noticed Preston and Frank again in a huddle. Preston looked up and caught his eye: he held the glare for a moment and then got up off the bench he sat on and sauntered up to Duncan, his eyebrows drawn together in the familiar scowl. "What're you looking at, Shrimp?"

"Not much, Fatso." Duncan signed his name on a ticket for a ten-cent candy bar.

"You've got a funny look on your face I don't much like the look of," Preston growled.

"I can't help what my face looks like. If we could pick our own face, you'd never have picked yours." He bit the candy bar in two and chewed it up, feeling pretty good about that crack.

"Don't get smart with me, New Boy."

"Ha! I'm not a new boy any more."

"I'll call you as I see you, New Boy." Preston glowered a step closer and his voice dropped low. "And I just better not have to call you 'stool pigeon.'"

Duncan lurched on the inside and involuntarily his eyes widened a little as he realized suddenly that Preston had read his mind correctly, just as *he* had correctly suspected a plot cooking between him and

Frank. "You know what I mean, don't you, New Boy?"

Duncan looked down at the fist between them, at the wart, cracked and dirty, that stood up tight on Preston's knuckle. He backed up a few steps. "Where'd you get that ugly-looking wart?"

Before lunch Duncan had a moment in private with Jeep. "You don't have to watch Preston any more, Jeep. I know for sure he's planning something."

"What're you going to do?" Jeep's blue eyes narrowed with worry.

"I don't know. But I'll think of something."

Duncan was at Frog Sifford's table that week. Bates sat on one side of him and Mark Bradley on the other. "What kind of fireworks do we got for tonight?" Bates asked eagerly.

"All kinds." Frog smiled as he served the plates with meat loaf, mashed potatoes, and gravy.

"Who gets to shoot 'em off?"

"Don, I guess. He did it last year." That was bad news to Duncan. Don wouldn't be able to keep track of his cabin.

"I'd sure like to help him; doesn't he need an assistant?"

Everyone but Duncan clamored that they wanted to help light the fuses, and Frog finally waved his hand and said, "All of you pipe down." Duncan wished Preston could be appointed. It would be an honor he didn't deserve, but at least it would keep him and his matches out of the woods.

"Don't you like firecrackers?" Mark asked Duncan, his freckled pink face tilted up.

"Sure, but you can see better from the shore."

"That's right," Frog said. "I'm glad I'll be on the beach with the watchers. There'll be two counselors on the float and Uncle Murdock will get some campers to stand by in canoes."

Now there was a possibility! "How come?" Duncan asked, his mouth full of mashed potatoes.

"In case of fire. Remote chance, but if a rocket didn't go off on time and lit on the beach still spewing, the canoes could be there quickly to prevent any spread of sparks to the woods."

"How do you get to be appointed?"

"That's up to Uncle Murdock."

The little bell tinkled and everyone looked toward the head table. Uncle Murdock pushed his chair back and heaved himself up. A spot of gravy stained the front of his big T shirt. He smiled around at everyone and everyone smiled back. "Guess what?" he said. Nobody guessed. Everyone held his breath. Uncle Murdock's announcements were always good news. "We're having a cookout tonight before the celebration."

Clapping and drumming with feet on the floor

broke out spontaneously. Uncle Murdock raised his hand and silence came quickly. The cookout would be at the archery field. The boys would build their own fires and cook shish kebabs. "I'll ask the Panthers to report to the kitchen at five thirty," Uncle Murdock said, "to load the food into the jeep and unload it at the field at each campfire location. The Wolves will be responsible for checking all campfires for safety and supplying each cabin with a bucket of lake water. And I want you Lions to carry the trash can from behind the infirmary to the archery field and see that all paper plates and napkins are put there before we return to the waterfront. Then we shall have a brilliant commemoration of the historic events of July 4, 1776."

Uncle Murdock took a deep breath and with his hand he made a motion like a rising sky rocket. "Today is the birthday of the United States of America, and this is how we shall celebrate." His fingers snapped out like a rocket bursting into sparks. "As an added precaution against fire, I will ask some boys to patrol the shore in canoes, lest some delinquent spark gets loose . . ."

Before Uncle Murdock could finish talking, hands quivered in the air and everyone was loudly whispering, "Me, me, me." Duncan's hand shot up too as an idea burst into his mind like a rocket going off. He leaned in front of Bates and took hold of Frog

Sifford's arm and shook it. "Frog, Frog! I've got a great idea. He ought to appoint the winners of last night's canoe races, the fastest paddlers, if a fire broke out!"

Frog nodded approval; his thumb and finger together aimed a circle at Duncan. He stood up and got Uncle Murdock's attention. "We had such a good suggestion at this table, Uncle Murdock, that I thought you'd like to hear it. You could reward the winners of last night's canoe races with this appointment."

"Excellent idea, Frog! Would the winners of the races stand up, please, so I can see you?"

Duncan turned half around in his chair and cast a glance at Preston. Preston met that glance with an icy grimace. His elbows spread out on the table, he pressed his fists together like rams' heads. Duncan was exuberant! What a simple solution to the problem. It was as if he had put out a fire in the forest with only a squirt gun.

"Preston, you came in third," the first winner said; "stand up." Preston dragged himself up, looking glum.

"All right," Uncle Murdock said, "you boys pick a buddy and be out at the raft tonight at eight o'clock."

The Secret Hideout

Duncan's letters home had been short, but now, on the third Sunday, he was writing a long one. He had a private hideout on the edge of the cove, he said. He had paddled there once in a canoe with his best friend, Jeep, but recently he had found a way to get there on foot.

Now he sat with his pencil and paper on a thick pad of pine needles and leaned back against a tree. He could see everything in the cove that moved. Frogs and lizards climbed on the dead tree that slanted down the bank into the water. A fun thing he liked to do was shoot his squirt gun at these creatures. It didn't scare them; they probably thought it was rain; it sure hadn't rained in a long time.

The best thing about the cove was that a big king snake stayed around it, especially in the branches of the fallen tree. It had got used to him, he wrote, and slid away only when he tried to pick it up.

He decided not to mention in the letter that he had a bad case of poison ivy, or the friction burn on his arm from archery. He said his tennis had improved so much that he sometimes beat Tully two games out of six. He started a new page. "Fireworks on the Fourth of July were great. Rockets lit things up brighter than the moon, and you could see the boys in canoes paddling around. The next day one of the guys in our cabin shot off some cherry bombs in the archery field, but he got caught. Uncle Murdock made another speech about forest fires. You'd like Uncle Murdock, Dad, except that he's narrow-minded about snakes."

Duncan put down his notebook and pencil. The snake was there. It had quietly slipped up in the branches of the tree while he was writing the letter. Slowly, Duncan climbed down the bank and out on the log, his bare feet lightly touching the muddy bottom as he straddled the log. Gradually, with no quick movements, he inched himself out till he was close to the place where the log went under water. The snake was overhead, coiled around the dead limbs, close enough for Duncan to see in detail the black scales and the pale yellow bands like links in a chain. The snake looked at Duncan with curious round black eyes. Its forked tongue flickered in and out. There was a lump in its body that wasn't there before . . . probably a frog, they were so plentiful.

For several minutes Duncan and the snake eyed each other as Duncan slowly raised his hand. His heart pounded. He could, if he chose to, catch the snake. But not now. Next Sunday he'd come back with the zipper case. The snake began to unwind. "I wouldn't hurt you," Duncan said softly. Slowly it dipped into the water and swam to shore where it disappeared among the low bushes.

Duncan dropped his letter in the mailbox by the store in the lodge. Then he went to the Nature Hut to feed the creatures in his terrarium a few bugs he had caught. He brought out of his pocket a Cracker Jack box containing two grasshoppers and one beetle. He dropped a grasshopper and a beetle under the wire and watched quietly as the biggest toad flicked out his tongue and polished off the grasshopper in a gulp. It took longer for Murdock, the fence lizard, to get around the beetle. He had to do some chewing.

Duncan had Holy to thank for the wash-tub terrarium. He had taken him to a little country town in the jeep two Saturdays ago to buy the tub and the screen to go on top. Together they planted it with moss and various leafy plants. The six toads in it often soaked in the sunken pool, made from a tuna fish can, but the fence lizard stayed dry. He got water only from the juicy bugs Duncan and Holy provided.

Now Duncan unscrewed the punctured lid of a peanut butter jar and dropped in the other grasshopper. This praying mantis he had caught was the weirdest, most fascinating insect Duncan had ever had. At mealtimes especially it put on a real show. Daintily, on its dry branch, the color of itself, it twisted its triangular head around on its slender stalk and looked down at the grasshopper, then back at Duncan as if to say, "Thank you." Then its crab-like arms began waving, as if it were gracefully, in slow motion, going through some sort of ceremony praying mantises performed before eating. The grasshopper jumped against the glass and the mantis scurried down the branch, carrying its fat body high on its thin, jointed legs. Its delicate pincers embraced the grasshopper so it couldn't move; and lapping its chops, its tiny mandibles, its eyes bulging, it prepared to eat the victim alive. At the bottom of the jar were the wings of many devoured moths and the brittle discarded legs of grasshoppers.

But something was different about this meal, Duncan realized almost immediately. The mantis just couldn't get started. Usually it bit a neat hole in the body of the bug it embraced and slowly, like eating an apple, continued till it was down to the distasteful parts. Then like a cat the mantis would lick its paws and wipe its face. But this praying mantis, instead of eating the grasshopper, was licking it! "Holy, take a look at this crazy mantis," Duncan said, carrying the peanut butter jar into the Nature Hut.

Holy looked at it and agreed. It sure had gone nuts. They watched it silently for quite a while. Occasionally the mantis would look up at them and grin, it seemed. Finally Holy asked, "Say, Duncan, did you have honey on your hands when you caught that grasshopper?"

"No, but . . ." He ran outside and came back with the Cracker Jack box. "I put it in this. Do mantises like sweet stuff?"

Holy looked in the box. "That's what it is all right. That grasshopper's covered with caramel syrup."

"Well I'll be . . . He likes Cracker Jack!"

The grasshopper dropped to the bottom of the jar and flopped around. The old moth wings rustled like dead rose petals. Up on its perch the praying mantis fastidiously groomed the hairs on its jointed arms.

"Why didn't you come to practice?" Preston demanded as Duncan came up the path to the cabin.

"We got beat by Racoon," Sid said.

"Where were you?" Preston blocked the path. His dark straight hair clung damply to his forehead, almost covering one eye.

"I was looking for bugs for my collection."

"You should have been at the game."

"I don't have to play when it's free time."

"This was a scheduled game."

"Who scheduled it?"

"I did."

"That doesn't count. It wasn't posted."

"Stupidest thing I ever heard, collecting bugs," Preston sneered.

"I don't collect bugs. I collect creatures that *eat* bugs."

"What kind of creatures?"

"Toads, for instance." He knew that would get a snort from Preston.

"Toads," Preston snorted. "Stupidest thing I ever heard, collecting toads."

Duncan ducked around Preston and ran up the steps to the cabin. "I happen to like toads."

"Only sissies like that kind of stuff."

Pete and Joe, who lay side by side on Joe's bed, frowned behind the *Superman* comic they shared. Tully, drying his hands on a towel, came out of the bathroom as if he had lost something and was trying to find it mixed in with the clothes on his shelf. Frank and Sid stood on the porch looking through the screen door. Jeep, who had been playing a game of solitaire on his bed, stopped laying out the cards and bit his fingernails. Duncan sat on his bed, knowing he was red in the face.

He visualized himself making a bound up from there, his fists swinging, aimed at Preston's stomach, high up where he was always telling guys to sock him, when he was ready and the muscle was hard as a rock and he wanted to show off how tough he was. Duncan would get him when the muscle was soft, and he'd fold like a knife. And what would happen next? Preston would knock him out cold, no doubt, but worse than that, much worse, for starting a fight, he'd be disqualified for the Caneechee "C." Duncan wanted that "C." It would be a badge of honor.

"That kid is chicken," Preston crowed, swaggering over to Tully, who, looking confused, went back to the bathroom, still drying his hands.

On the way down to supper, Jeep said, "Did you get close enough to touch the snake today, Dunc?"

"I could have, but I'm not going to try to catch him till Sunday. I just watched him, and he watched me. If I worry him he might go away. Anyway, I wouldn't have any place to keep him."

"Holy wouldn't tell. You could leave him at nature."

"But somebody'd find him; then everybody would know."

Jeep tossed a pine cone up in the air and laughed. "Hey, just imagine the ruckus if you brought him into the cabin . . ."

". . . and put him in Preston's bed," Duncan snickered.

Jeep let out a yelp and caught Duncan by the arm. "Do it, Duncan, do it. Really do it, that's a great idea! Boy, oh, boy, I can just see Preston scared out of his wits, yelling bloody murder, his hair standing up like a wire brush and his knees buckling beneath him." Jeep, whose snow-white hair had grown so long that it covered the tips of his pink ears, hopped around, hooting lustily.

"Jeep, you idiot, that's a horrible idea. It's the poor *snake* that would be scared out of his wits. He'd fall off the bed and probably whack himself into the screen door. He'd be petrified. And some fool would be sure to make a hero out of himself by hitting him with a baseball bat."

Jeep sobered down. "Well, anyway, I'd like to see Preston get wiped out."

"Me too."

Jeep's Ordeal

THE LAST WEEK of camp seemed to race by. It was already Friday. Every night after supper had been spent at the Craft Shop or rehearsing for the drama. Duncan had lavishly decorated his Indian costume and had made a beaded belt like Uncle Murdock's for his father. For his mother he modeled out of clay a bird in a bird bath. When it was baked the yellow beak ran into the red and the red had leaked into the blue of the fluted bowl. But he liked it anyway, and he knew his mother would.

In the drama Duncan was one of the bad Indians. He looked forward to tomorrow when at the dress rehearsal he could paint his face and chest with war paint. Tonight's practice was just over now. It was already dark; he pulled on his sweat shirt and headed for the cabin. Day after tomorrow his par-

138

ents would arrive and seat themselves with the other parents on the lawn to watch the drama of winning the peace between the pioneer settlers and the Indians. In the final act, after the dancing and preparation for war was changed to a Harvest Festival, Duncan would fly into the peaceful scene with the other stubborn braves and swing his tomahawk around, hooting his loudest. And then, in a moment of glory, he would be slain. He and Sid, a good settler, had practiced the final contest with the help of some of Perry's judo techniques and had it dramatically perfected. After the killing, he would lie in a heap with the other bad Indians and, panting from his strenuous exertions, he would listen to the talk of the peacemakers as they passed the peace pipe from one to another, puffing up a cloud of real smoke from Uncle Murdock's real Indian ceremonial pipe.

He went around the back of the cabin, climbed the water tank and up to the roof. Since Don had said it was all right to climb trees, Duncan had got in the habit of climbing the big pine tree whenever there was a little time to waste. He liked the view from up there, and when he was hot, he liked the breeze. Most of the intermediate boys had gone up and down that tree a few times when the word got out that it was permissible.

Now he was up near the moon. Down below were

the boys slowly climbing the hill in the light of the bulbs strung along the path. The fronts of the cabins were lit by floodlights. Jeep lay on the broad rounded railing of Bear Cabin porch. Duncan smiled and knew what Jeep was thinking. Just two more days and he'd see his pony again. He sure loved that pony. Everyone was relaxed after the rehearsal and no one was talking. So Jeep's high voice carried up to Duncan in the tree. "This is how I lie on my pony while he's grazing," he said.

Suddenly Preston leaped up the steps and slapped the log behind Jeep. "I'll whack your pony on the rump and he'll run away and break his leg in a gopher hole!"

Duncan clutched the trunk of the tree tighter. That detestable Preston! The scene below was lively now. "Let's horse fight," Preston yelled. "Come on, Pete." Pete jumped on Preston's back and they galloped in a circle in the clearing.

"Charge," cried Joe, who was up on Tully.

Jeep sat erect on the railing, his hands out flat, thumb to thumb. His white hair was like another spotlight gleaming down below. Then he leaped over the bushes, calling Frank. The scream he let out was too high and piercing; it raised gooseflesh on Duncan's arms. Pete dragged Joe from his horse and he lay on the ground laughing. Jeep locked his legs around Frank's waist. A cloud of dust rose up

as they circled around Pete and Preston. "Charge!" Jeep screamed. The riders grappled; they swayed together in a fierce embrace. Frank backed away, but Jeep spurred him on, yelling, "Charge!" He caught Pete around the neck and dragged him backwards till Pete let go with his feet and dropped to the ground. Then Jeep grabbed Preston around the neck. "Hey, you got the horse," someone yelled and laughed.

Jeep's sun-burned face seemed redder than it ever had and his white head bobbed up and down as the three of them tilted around, surrounded by a cheering, laughing audience. Then all three fell in a heap. Frank stood up, laughing, brushing the dust off his pants. But Preston rolled over on Jeep, pinned him

to the ground, one knee on his chest. He picked up
a handful of dust and rubbed it into Jeep's hair. Jeep
thrashed and kicked. Several boys pulled Preston off.
Jeep leaped to his feet. "You bully! You stupid
bully!" he screamed. His head was thrust forward
and his clenched hands stuck out behind him. "You
stupid bully, I wish I was big enough to knock your
block off. Then we'd find out it's *you* that's chicken."

"Who're you calling chicken?" Preston shook loose
of the boys who had pulled him off Jeep.

"You!" Jeep screamed. "I . . . I . . . I wish you'd
get bit by a cottonmouth moccasin!"

Duncan's heart pounded as he heard the dead
silence down below. Quickly he came down from
his high perch. "Now look who's stupid," Preston
jeered. "There aren't any snakes around here."

"Yes, there are!"

"No, there aren't."

"Yes, there are. I've *seen* one."

In the floodlights all faces turned to Jeep; silence
hung in the air like dust. "What'd you say?"

"I . . . I . . . there *are* snakes around here. Don
said so."

"You said you *saw* one." Jeep backed into the
crowd, but Preston caught him by the arm and
dragged him inside the circle of light. "You're a
liar," he said.

"I am not."

"Then you *did* see a snake. You said you saw a cottonmouth moccasin."

"No, I didn't."

"Liar!" Preston swung to the crowd. "He *did* say it, didn't he."

"No, I didn't."

"Yes, you did. Where was it, Jeep? Where did you see the snake?"

Duncan dropped from the roof of the cabin to the ground with a jolt that rattled his teeth. He fell into a tree, scraping his ear on the bark. He couldn't see Jeep any more, but he heard the rising, excited voices, and when he burst through the circle, Preston had Jeep backed up against a tree, his hand at his throat.

Preston let go and Jeep fell to the ground, gasping for breath. At that moment, Don, who had been running up the hill, pushed his way through the crowd of boys. "What's going on here?" he demanded. Jeep staggered to his feet, yelling at Preston, "You stupid, stupid bully." But Preston had disappeared.

Jeep's hair was the color of dust. Don put his arm around him and led him toward the cabin. "What started it, Jeep? You know fighting's no way to settle things."

"I'd like to knock his big stupid block off!"

"What happened, Jeep?" But Jeep just shook his

head and wiped his sweaty face on his arm, smearing the dirt. Don's face was stern, but he patted Jeep gently on his dusty head. "Go wash your face, Jeep. I'll talk to you later." He went out, letting the screen door slam.

"Did you tell him about the snake, Jeep?" Duncan asked.

Jeep hit the door to the bathroom with the heel of his hand; it swung back and banged into the wall. "I hate him, I hate him, I hate him!"

"Did you tell him where the snake was, Jeep?"

Jeep let out a groan. "I'm sorry, darn it all, Dunc. I was so mad and he just about twisted my head off. He had me by the throat and my arm pinned against the tree, and his horrible eyes about two inches from my face. I should have spit at him!"

"Did you tell him *where*, Jeep?"

"Yes, darn it, I told. Oh gosh . . ." Jeep's voice wavered almost into a sob. He spun toward the sink, turned on the water full blast, and ducked his whole head into it. "Dumb, stupid Preston," he mumbled. The water turned brown and Jeep's hair came out white again and standing on end like the hair of a wet dog.

"Forget Preston," Duncan said. "He's a grubby rat."

Jeep covered his head with a towel and continued

to mumble. ". . . grubby, dumb, stupid, blasted rat."

"I don't know what'll happen if Uncle Murdock finds out," Duncan said, "but I'm sure not going to let anybody get that snake."

"I'll help you catch it, Duncan."

From one who was as afraid of snakes as Jeep was, that was a generous offer. But Duncan could do it better alone, he said. They'd wait and see what came of the now common knowledge that a snake was in the cove, and then make plans.

The Snake Hunt

THE STORY of an enormous cottonmouth moccasin in the cove spread like a brush fire. At breakfast, even as they stood behind their chairs before the blessing, everyone spoke of it in whispers. At Duncan's table, Gooch said he'd heard about this snake last night from Don, and before reveille at Uncle Murdock's suggestion, he had gone in a canoe to check it out. Every eye was glued to Gooch. Yes, he'd seen the snake. "It slithered up a log that lay in the water and hung itself in loops in the branches. It was *this* big around." He clasped his forearm. Someone suggested it might be a pregnant female. Then, of course, its mate was sure to be around.

One of the seniors told what he knew about the teeth of some kind of venomous snake: they were hollow and they bent backward and when the snake bit a person it shot out poison through its teeth. "The baby ones are poisonous too," he added.

Duncan wanted to laugh out loud, to tell them they were all wet, that there was only one snake, and it was a king snake no bigger than his own forearm, nowhere near as big as Gooch's, and what a lot of stupid worry they were working up to over one harmless snake that wasn't about to bite anybody and wanted only to be left in peace. But he decided it was best to be quiet. What he hoped was that since camp was almost over, they'd plan to wait till the boys were gone to get rid of the snake. They'd plan to do it before the new group of boys came in for the second session. Duncan smiled to himself. They'd never find that snake. Sunday it would be in his zipper bag.

Uncle Murdock tinkled the bell and everyone was quiet. He had a special announcement. And, of course, it was about the snake. He said how sorry he was to hear of the presence of a large snake in the cove. But there was to be no more worry about it. He said that during dress rehearsal for the drama that night, some of the counselors would go to the cove and kill the snake.

Duncan's heart leaped to his throat. Every boy

whispered to his neighbor; a low buzz of excitement swelled up to the rafters of the dining hall. Uncle Murdock motioned for silence with widespread arms. And then, with his hands flat on the white tablecloth he leaned forward, hunched toward the listening boys and counselors, in an attitude quite different from Uncle Murdock's usual erect posture. "There are those here who would let this snake go free," he began in his sonorous voice, "free as the other creatures of the woods. And to them . . ." he looked at Duncan ". . . I owe these words, which are painful for me. They are my personal confession of an old guilt." Again Duncan felt the tingle of gooseflesh induced by Uncle Murdock's poetic powers. Hunched there, Uncle Murdock looked over the heads of everyone to the back of the room, his immense size seeming strangely cramped by his humble stance. "At Camp Caneechee many years ago, when some of your dads were here as boys, a disaster occurred, a disaster which stamped upon my heart an unalterable sorrow. A child in my care was bitten by a poisonous snake, and in our infirmary, he died." Duncan couldn't even breathe. "Thereafter we have been meticulous to clear these grounds of the dread possibility that such a tragedy could again strike."

So this was the cause of Uncle Murdock's terrible fear of snakes! There was no unlocking so deep a prejudice. Nothing that he, a boy of twelve, could say would show Uncle Murdock that his fear was foolish, that this snake was not a threat.

Throughout the meal everyone talked about killing the snake. Duncan couldn't eat. His mind grasped out in all directions for a plan, a way to get out of classes without being missed so he could catch the snake before *they* did. And as he nibbled the crust of his toast and stared into his glass of milk, a ruse occurred to him; it slipped into his mind as deftly as a hummingbird lighting on a twig. He reached down, a smile on his face, and scratched his old poison ivy scabs.

On his way out of the dining room, Duncan beckoned to Jeep who came over, frowning his white eyebrows together. Duncan pointed down at his legs and grinned. "Look."

"Good grief, I thought it was all dried up!"

"It was, but now it's bad again, for some reason." He twisted his face in a grimace of pain, and then laughed. "Do you think Don'll let me go to the infirmary at rest period?"

Jeep grinned suddenly. "Oh, I get it. Heck yes, he will. You look terrible. What would you like me to do?"

"Just tell anybody that asks how bad off I am."

After lunch Duncan got Don's permission to go have his poison ivy doctored, and with a pillow slip folded under his belt, he set out for the infirmary. At the fork in the trail, he looked around, and, seeing no one, broke into a run along the path to the Council Ring. He sailed over bushes, under branches and vines, and straight through the poison ivy patch. At the edge of the cove, he took off his shoes, his heart racing and sad. He had deceived Don. He'd rather have confided in him, but Don might have stopped him. He pulled out the pillow slip and spread it over a broken branch, open at the top. Slowly, he let himself out on the log and straddled the trunk just up from the wet part, his feet resting on the mud bottom.

It seemed a long time that he waited. Rest period was probably over and tennis was soon to begin. But he couldn't worry about that. There was a stir among the cattails. Yes! It was the snake, its head like a stick, weaving through the water, leaving a trail of ripples.

Duncan sat like part of the log as the snake swam directly toward him, past his knee. It lifted its head and coiled up into the low branches. Its movements were relaxed, its tongue flickered, and the trusting round eyes looked at him. He wished he didn't have to disturb it. But there wasn't time to waste. Both hands darted out and caught the snake behind the head and in the middle of the body. He wasn't prepared for the struggle that followed. His heels dug into the muddy bottom and the seat of his pants slipped forward on the algae-covered wet log. Like a rider bareback, he was thrown. He gasped as he lit on his back in the water, the snake thrashing above him, jerking his arms in and out. Water was in his nose; he choked and sputtered, his legs deep in the slimy mud. Nothing mattered but holding on. His fingers were loose but firm around the snake. His arms ached. On his knees he crawled onto the solid shore and stood up, talking softly to the snake. "I wouldn't hurt you, boy, I wouldn't hurt you. Just calm down, it's okay." His voice was slow and monotonous. It had always been a good voice for soothing snakes. The snake became calm in his hands, its tail wrapped around his upper arm. "See, I told you. Everything's okay. I'm going to save your life." With a sigh of relief he lowered the snake into the open pillow case and tied a knot in the top.

His shirt and pants were slick with mud. He'd have to clean up before he went back. He took off his clothes and rinsed them in the lake, then put them back on. When he had washed his legs and put on his shoes, he picked up the pillow case and the quiet snake and walked slowly into the woods.

Now, where was he going to hide it? He couldn't risk taking it back to the cabin, but the white pillow case was too conspicuous just to leave under a bush. If the counselors came over here during rehearsal looking for the snake, they'd notice something white and naturally they'd think about trash belonging in trash cans. Duncan chuckled over the thought that came to mind of how Gooch would calmly reach under a bush for this piece of trash. Yipe! a snake! He'd about jump out of his skin when the snake began to wiggle.

A good idea, the trash can. He could put it in a trash can. No one ever used the one by the infirmary excepts for cookouts at the archery field. He began to run over the springy ground, cradling the snake in his arms. It was still, as if already tame. He felt like shouting and singing, *The snake is safe!* He cut through the Council Ring and down to the fork in the trail. No one saw him, he made sure. He took the lid off the can, lowered the snake into it, and replaced the cover.

At top speed he dashed down the path, his clothes drying in the wind. He swung up the steps of Bear Cabin wanting to laugh, to let out a Tarzan yell louder than any that had ever been heard. He let the door slam. Why do it softly? Oh, summer sun and squirt gun fights! Never had he ever felt such absolute, total, complete . . . *unsmushable* triumph. But he got a hold on the crazy things he wanted to do and say. It wouldn't do to draw too much attention to himself. Somebody might get too inquisitive and he'd be forced into an outright lie.

"What happened to you?" Pete asked.

Duncan peeled off his shirt and pants, giving Pete a big grin. "I fell in the creek."

"I thought you went to the infirmary."

Duncan ran to the bathroom with the bottle of calamine lotion Dr. Madison had given him two weeks ago. In private he smeared his legs with the gooey pink stuff, covering the old scabs newly encrusted with dirt.

He was in clean clothes and stretched on his bed pretending to read Pete's *Superman* comic when Tully and Frank came in. "Why weren't you at tennis?" Frank asked.

"I was supposed to go to the infirmary."

Tully came over and looked at Duncan's legs. "Ga, you sure got a bad case."

Duncan managed a look of mild pain. Inside he was about to fold up laughing. "It sure itches."

"I bet it does." Tully pulled Duncan's little toe gently. "That'll teach you to goof off looking for bugs."

"It wasn't bugs this time, Tully, it was crawdads." Pete giggled. "He fell in the creek."

Duncan scowled sternly. "Pete, do you have to tell everything you know?"

"We missed our doubles game 'cause you weren't there," Frank said. "Was Preston ever mad."

"Sorry," Duncan said.

"Yeh, I'll bet." Preston slammed in the door. "You haven't got any team spirit. I bet if Don let us, you wouldn't even go after that snake either."

"You want to bet? I'd just love to pick up that snake and take him home for a pet." Naturally, Preston didn't know of Duncan's experience with snakes. He had told only Don and Jeep.

Preston planted himself by the bed, looking scornfully down at Duncan. "Boy, do you talk big. A chicken like you would run a mile from a snake, even if you had on a suit of armor."

Duncan burst out laughing, he couldn't help it. The *Superman* comic jiggled up and down on his stomach. "It'd sure be hard for a chicken to run a mile in a suit of armor!"

Preston jerked the comic out of Duncan's hands and threw it across the room. "You louse up our doubles contest and then smart off about it. You're getting pretty far out on a limb, Shrimp."

"Make up your mind, am I a shrimp or a chicken?" Duncan propped himself up on one elbow, absolutely unable to stop smiling.

Preston clenched his fists, took a deep breath and a step closer. "You're chicken, Shrimp. Look at the fuss you make over a little poison ivy, have to run to the doctor." He sneered contemptuously.

"He's got a bad case, Preston," Tully said.

"You stay out of this, Tully. What I said was, he's

chicken, and I dare him to prove otherwise." Just how this could be proved one way or the other, Duncan didn't know, unless Preston was challenging him to start a fight. And *that* he would never do. "He wouldn't have the nerve to kill that snake if he had a club in his hands and it was sound asleep with its eyes closed."

"Snakes don't close their eyes when they sleep, Preston. They have a little transparent flap over them. But you're right, I wouldn't kill it. I'd leave it alone."

"You bet you would, you'd give it a wide berth."

"Yup." Duncan pressed his lips together tightly to keep back the laughter that tumbled around inside him. He ached to laugh. He felt reckless and invincible. Nothing that happened from now on could matter—he had saved the snake. It was an enormous secret. If Preston wanted to fly into a rage, let him. He wouldn't mind too much even being dragged up off the bed and knocked out cold.

"You're darn right you'd be scared." Preston was halfway through the swinging door into the bathroom when Duncan called him to a halt.

"Hey, Preston. D'ya want to know what I'd like to do to that snake?"

Preston turned on his heel. "What?"

"I'd like to shoot him with my squirt gun."

Preston came back slowly, leaning slightly forward like a gorilla; his arms hung down straight from his shoulders and his eyes were small black angry buttons. His disheveled hair made sharp peaks all over his head. He glared down at Duncan. "You're cracking up," he growled. "You'd shoot a deadly poisonous snake with a squirt gun?"

Duncan lifted one arm and took aim at Preston. He pulled an imaginary trigger. "Splaaat!" Then his hand flopped down on his stomach and he laughed so hard he had Tully, Frank, and Pete all nervously laughing too.

Preston's broad shoulders heaved as he rocked up and down on his heels. His thumbs hung in his pockets. His eyebrows puckered in a frown over his flinty eyes. "You just wait, McKenna!" He turned on his heel and slammed into the bathroom. This was something new. The sound of his own last name hissed through Preston's teeth had an ominous ring that was sobering.

Jeep came softly in the door and over to Duncan's bed. "What're you trying to do, Duncan? Get yourself killed?"

"I don't care if he gets mad," Duncan said, loud enough for Preston to hear through the swinging door. "He's chicken. And he's a grubby, dumb, stupid bully."

Everyone in the cabin hardly breathed, their eyes on the bathroom door. But the door stayed closed.

The Showdown

D U N C A N S A T on the grass watching a badminton
game in front of the lodge before dress rehearsal.
Gooch came out of the garage with an assortment
of hoes and shovels and joined Don on the shore.
On the way to supper, Don, with his arm around
Duncan's shoulder, had gently assured him that
Gooch was sure the snake was a cottonmouth and
therefore ought to be done away with for the safety
of the boys in the second session of camp. He
seemed relieved that Duncan didn't protest and
beg to be allowed to go along with his book of
snakes to make a positive identification.

Four counselors wearing jeans took three canoes

158

down from the racks and set them in the water. Then they had a conference with Don and Gooch who went away, returning in a few minutes dressed in jeans. Gooch had on a pair of boots and another pair he held in his hands. All six of the counselors seemed in high spirits, joking about who was to get the extra pair of boots. Frog Sifford apparently had the biggest feet.

It was a little sad, Duncan felt, to watch these good guys that he had come to like so much doing this stupid thing. But how impossible it would have been for him to set them straight. Even his book of snakes, with all its facts, wouldn't convince them. They wouldn't read it. They still would want to kill the snake. Well, let them search.

It was his turn at badminton. As he leaped and slammed the bird around he thought out the rest of his plan. Tomorrow, after the performance of the play, he and his mother and father would go to the trash can and transfer the snake into his zipper bag. It might have got out of the pillow case through a hole or a weak seam, but it couldn't escape from the can.

The bird whizzed under his racket and the game was over. The winner slapped him on the back. "Let's go get our paint on," he said. They skinned off their shirts as they ran to the Craft Shop. Duncan glanced back and saw the three canoes with the six men paddling swiftly on the orange lake.

With paint dripping from the brush, Duncan drew on himself white skeleton ribs. It tickled. On his chest he painted two yellow spirals and edged them in blue. In the center, just over the top of his fringed loincloth he painted a red heart pierced by a black arrow. He felt almost naked in this costume that left a bare streak from the string at his waist down the side of his leg.

It was hard to stand still he was so happy. To-morrow he'd see his mother and dad, and there'd be a snake to take home, plus Murdock, the fat fence lizard, the praying mantis, and the toads. The toads would end up as food for the museum's baby alligator. King snakes didn't like toads. He'd have to set his Havahart trap in the woods and catch some mice or chipmunks for the king snake.

He flexed his arm muscles, and the stripes of red, yellow, and black, in series like the bands of a coral snake, lurched, making the other boys laugh and try it themselves. He glared into the mirror and painted yellow frown lines. Black on his eyelids made his eyes look sunken and grim. His nose became a broad red triangle with a yellow center stripe. His jaw was bright blue. No matter how much he laughed at the mirror, he still looked horrible and fierce.

When rehearsal was over, almost everyone ran to the shore to see if the counselors had returned with the snake. Duncan sat on the railing of the lodge and watched the canoes being pulled up on the sand and inverted over the racks.

Uncle Murdock came up behind Duncan and put his big hand on Duncan's shoulder. Duncan looked up and smiled, feeling the paint crackle on his skin. "My, you're a primeval-looking specimen," Uncle Murdock said.

"They didn't bring any snake back," Duncan said.

"They'll try again tomorrow," Uncle Murdock said. "You understand, don't you, Duncan, why this has to be? I know, with a background such as yours, your father being curator of a Nature Museum, it would be natural for you to want to capture this snake alive. But we must think of our commitment to safety."

"Actually, Uncle Murdock, it's probably a king snake. Don told me they got some of that kind at pre-camp, and it would be a very good idea to have a few king snakes around here, for the safety of the campers, if you're worried about snake bites. King snakes eat the poisonous kind. They squeeze 'em to death and swallow 'em whole. I saw one do it once." Duncan had Uncle Murdock's rapt attention. "They put a copperhead in with a king snake by mistake. The king snake was curled up out of sight in a hollow log and this helper of my father's thought it was an empty cage. It took sixteen hours for him to swallow the whole thing." Uncle Murdock's face looked paler and looser. He pulled at his chin, making the dent deeper. "Fantastic!" he murmured, shaking his big head slowly back and forth. "That copperhead was even bigger than the king snake, too, Uncle Murdock. You really ought to have a few king snakes around to keep away any stray rattlers or copperheads. Sort of like keeping a few watch dogs."

Uncle Murdock opened and closed his mouth a few times. "But, Duncan, this snake is reported to be a venomous cottonmouth moccasin."

Duncan shook his head and smiled. "Uncle Murdock, you can't believe everything you hear. There *aren't* any cottonmouths this far north."

For a few more moments Uncle Murdock stared down at Duncan. "Fantastic," he said again and, still pulling at his chin, he turned away. At the top of the steps he blew his whistle and took down the megaphone. "Council Fire in ten minutes," he announced. "Indians, please wash your faces."

For a few seconds Duncan sat stunned by the announcement. How could he have forgotten Council Fire? It was the high point of the week. The last two days had been so snarled up with the problem of the snake, it had completely slipped his mind. And this was award night, too. If he had remembered, he'd have moved the can back, away from the trail. It wasn't often used, but there was a chance.

Jeep was crossing the bridge. He had changed his settler's coat for a sweater. "Jeep!" Duncan shouted, and ran to catch up with him. "Come help me move that can," he whispered breathlessly.

"Where you hid the snake?"

Duncan nodded. They broke into a run toward the infirmary. "I forgot about Council Fire. Somebody might find him."

But already they were too late. Here came Corn Flakes and a band of little campers, dallying up the trail. They scuffed in the dust and tapped the

can with their hands when they passed it. To move
it now would only attract attention to it. "Nobody
ever uses that can, Dunc."

"Yeh, but what if they did?"

"You've got to wash your face and you don't even
have a sweat shirt."

"I can't help it; I'd better stay here, just in case.
Why don't you go save me a seat, Jeep. Here comes
Preston."

Everyone was fed up with Preston. Bear Cabin
had lost at baseball and Preston kept rehashing
what everybody had done wrong. And since he
skipped the first rehearsal for the play, he had got
a bad part, a settler who said only one line and didn't
get to fight with the Indians. So during practices he
had goofed up everybody else's part, and nobody
thought he was even funny any more. Jeep ran up
the trail, arriving at the fork ahead of Preston, who
said something to Jeep, and then with a stick,
whacked the green trash can.

Duncan's heart lurched as he felt how that boom
would sound to the snake cowering inside. In a terrible flare-up of his imagination, he visualized Preston kicking the can over. The snake would roll out
on the ground in the pillow slip and thrash around
like the ghost of a dead rabbit! His teeth chattering
from the cold, he huddled in the bushes in his

scanty loin cloth and watched the orderly proces-
sion of boys, telling himself to simmer down, nothing
was going to happen to the snake.

When the line had passed safely by, he ran
around behind the log benches and wedged himself
in between Joe and Jeep. "Gosh, you're freezing,"
Jeep said. He took one arm out of his sweater and
stretched it around them both.

In the center of the ring the fire blazed toward
the moon, lighting every face with a warm, golden
glow. It was thrilling and a little sad to be singing
songs at the last Council Fire. Uncle Murdock called
on the counselors one by one, and each one went to
stand with his back to the roaring fire and call out
the names of boys who had won awards in the various activities. Wearing Jeep's sweater, Duncan went
up twice. He received a certificate for marksman-
ship in archery and the expert canoer's badge.

Then a third time his name was called. Brimming
over with joy, he again put on Jeep's sweater and
went up into the center of the ring for the "C" ceremony. Uncle Murdock winked at him and said in a
loud voice as he shook his hand, "I would never
have recognized my friend Duncan McKenna, except
that I have seen this fearsome mask before, and I
know it is he." Duncan smiled under the stiff paint,
warm with the knowledge that to Uncle Murdock

and the counselors he had proven himself to be a Caneechee camper of high moral principles, perseverance, and good sportsmanship. The fire crackled behind Uncle Murdock's white crest of hair. There was a long, quiet triumphant moment, and then applause.

When the winners of the "C"'s had been seated, Uncle Murdock walked around, smiling into everyone's face, his hands clasped over his broad stomach. The whistle rolled from side to side. He had a surprise, he said, a farewell token of his heartfelt love for each camper. Eskimo pies! Everyone cheered and raised the dust with stamping feet. Duncan was warm and happy snuggled next to Jeep inside the big sweater, the "C" in his hand, the "C" his mother would sew on a jacket. Nothing would taste better now than an Eskimo pie.

A large sealed carton was brought out of the woods where it had been hidden. It was ripped open with the fire tongs and a slab of dry ice was thrown into the fire, sending up a spray of sparks. Duncan wished he could have kept that dry ice. Gooch and Bagby passed the Eskimo pies. As he ate his, Duncan thought of things he'd like to do with the dry ice, if he had it. He would crack it up in little pieces and drop the pieces in a ginger ale bottle. Then he'd put in some water, cork it up and the pressure would build till the cork would pop like a cannonball. Also, he could put some in the john and it would burble like a boiling spring at Yellowstone Park.

Uncle Murdock's voice interrupted his speculations. "Two of you boys will please go get the trash can." Duncan was on his feet and running, the sweater sleeve wrong side out and dangling beside a startled Jeep. Two other boys got to the can before he did. They picked it up by the handles and carried it into the circle. Duncan stood panting beside it, staring at the lid, his brain in a whirl. The other boys sat down. Uncle Murdock held up his hand. "We'll close on the 'Caneechee Hymn,' boys. Then as you go out of the Council Ring, single file and in silence, drop your ice cream papers into the can. It's been a wonderful season, boys. Till next year, then, at the Council Fire, we will hold in our hearts a remembrance of good times we shared in the joy of being alive here in this pristine forest where the spirit of old Chief Eagle Feather hovers round." Then his deep bass voice led the singing of the "Caneechee Hymn."

"God of the mountains and the lake, whatever be Thy name,
Warm our hearts at the Council Fire with Thy steadfast flame."

Duncan's hand was on the lid of the can. Silently, he prayed, "Please, God, let no one see this snake."

Uncle Murdock motioned to him and he took the lid off. The mood of the hymn hung in the air as the campers filed past the can, dropping their ice cream wrappers into it. Duncan leaned over it and looked down to the dark bottom. There was the pillow slip, pale in the shadow. Also (his heart filled his chest so he could hardly breathe) the head of the snake, reaching up, wavering in and out of the small section made bright by the light of the moon.

A wadded-up piece of paper hit it and it dropped with a thud to the bottom of the can. Duncan's heart was a lead hammer pounding inside. The line seemed endless. Now here was Mark with a shy smile, lingering, his head hardly higher than the can. Duncan couldn't smile back. He looked at Mark and then back at the snake. Mark dropped his paper . . . then his eyes went round and he lurched backward with a piercing scream and grabbed Perry. "A snake! A snake!" he shrieked.

"Shut up!" Duncan snarled at him. The line of campers froze, all eyes riveted to the trash can. Mark sobbed and gasped in Perry's arms.

Uncle Murdock galloped up, his whistle swinging. He looked in the can, thrust Duncan back with his hand, picked up the lid, and slammed it on. He swayed unsteadily on his feet and, in a shaken voice, said, "Everyone back to the cabins." But no one moved, not even the counselors who had gathered around Uncle Murdock. Then a murmur came up from the campers on down the path; they swarmed through the trees into the circle to gather in a clot behind Uncle Murdock and the counselors.

Duncan couldn't think any more; he just stood there sweating, his hand on the top of the can, hearing the buzz of voices rise, watching the conference of the counselors and Uncle Murdock, waiting, he didn't know what for. Again he murmured, "Please, God, help me save this snake." And as he stood by the can, the feverish heat went away and he felt the cool air on his bare legs and his chest.

Uncle Murdock raised his hand. "All right, boys, I know you're all too keyed up to go to sleep till this is finished." Duncan didn't hear what else he said. Uncle Murdock picked up the fire tongs and the counselors went to the wood pile. "You boys get up on the benches. Duncan get back with the boys." Duncan didn't move. "Duncan, get back with the boys."

Duncan went up to Uncle Murdock. "Please don't kill him, Uncle Murdock; he's mine." Then he whirled and ran back to the can. "See, I'll show you." He took off the lid. With one swift stroke he caught the snake behind the head. It jerked and its body whacked the side of the can twice as he lifted it. With his other hand he caught it in the middle of the body. His arms were thrashed in and out till

finally he had the main weight of it pressed against his side under the red, yellow, and black bands on his upper arm. It was like holding a tommy gun, his trigger hand supporting the coils, the snake's head like the barrel of the gun in his other hand. It had stopped struggling now; only the tail moved, brushing softly against his bare leg. Duncan looked up and smiled. "See, Uncle Murdock, this snake is good."

Uncle Murdock's hand covered his mouth. His eyes fairly popped from his head and his white hair seemed to stand up on end. Behind him, in frozen postures of shock were the campers and counselors, their faces lit by the orange fire and the silver moon.

Duncan walked in a circle, adjusting the weight of the snake, enjoying the utter, dead silence, the undivided attention, knowing he was winning his point. Uncle Murdock stepped forward, the fire tongs held crossways like a quarterstaff. "For God's sake, Duncan, put it down, you'll get bitten!"

"He's not going to bite me, Uncle Murdock. This is a king snake. He eats poisonous snakes bigger than he is, but he won't bite me. I told you about king snakes, Uncle Murdock. They'd rather eat rattlesnakes than frogs. And he's tame. See, I'll prove it." He opened his hand. The snake's head rose up slowly beside Duncan's cheek. It brushed against his ear. Duncan lifted the coils to the level of his chest and the snake explored higher. It ruffled through Duncan's hair and paused a few moments on top of his head. Then its cool skin slipped lightly over his forehead as it came down the front way, the flickering tongue almost touching Duncan's nose. It settled back then, against the red heart on Duncan's stomach, and looked around at the stunned faces of the motionless boys and men.

"Duncan, Duncan," Uncle Murdock stammered, "put the snake in the can and put the lid on."

"I want to take him home with me."

"Put it in the can, please, Duncan."

"Someone might kill him. I want him for the museum collection."

"If your father wants it for the museum, he can have it."

"You won't let anyone kill him?" The snake's slender head wavered under Duncan's chin, the tongue flipping in and out.

"No, Duncan, no one will kill him. He's yours."

"Oh, thank you, Uncle Murdock, thanks a lot."

As he turned to put the snake in the can, the boys jumped off the benches and circled around at a cautious distance, reaching. "Let me see him, Duncan, let me see him."

"Get away, you'll scare him." Duncan backed up, colliding with someone behind him. He stumbled and the body of the snake slipped from under his arm and trailed to the ground. It began to jerk. "Take it easy, boy." Duncan caught it up again securely. Hands reached in all around, trying to touch the snake. "Darn you all, get back. Can't you see he's nervous? You can touch him when he's calmed down." He got down on one knee and rested the snake on the ground. Then with it neatly gathered, he stood up. The crowd continued to press around. He was almost at the can when he tripped over something and sprawled forward, unable he realized frantically, to catch his balance. One foot felt weighted to the ground. He let go of the snake and caught himself on his hands just before falling on it.

The snake took off, weaving through the dust, not fast, but curious, its head held high as it looked from side to side at the squealing boys, its tongue shivering in and out.

Then Duncan saw Preston, a chunk of firewood towering in his hands like a club. With a groan Duncan knew it all—what he had tripped over, who had nailed his foot down, unseen in all the commotion, and what was going to happen next. With hands like talons he threw himself at Preston, caught him by the back of his shirt and jerked, but not in time to keep the club from falling with a sickening thud, a death blow, Duncan knew, on the snake's back. The shirt ripped. With a sob, Duncan wrenched the club out of Preston's hand and slung it at him. Preston deflected it with a lift of his arm, and it slid into the Council Fire sending up an explosion of sparks. "You ugly wart!" Duncan attacked with clenched fists, but Preston's long arms stopped him, clamped him in the crook of his elbow, and scraped the crusty wart on the back of his neck. The touch of that wart was like a shot of adrenalin. He squirmed, slippery with sweat, and broke loose of the lock Preston held on his head. Blood drummed in his temples and stars spun around as he fell to the ground.

But almost instantly he was on his feet again. He leaped on Preston's back; with his forearm tight against Preston's throat, he locked his legs around his waist and jerked back and forth. Preston toppled sideways. Pain shot through Duncan's leg as Preston's weight came down on it. He lost the scissors hold. Jeering, Preston pinned him under his knee, as he had pinned Jeep before. Duncan's mouth was dry with dust and the taste of salt.

What mattered was to be on his feet, fighting this fight to the end. As he thrashed and bucked under Preston's knee, he heard his name called and a roar of voices. He grabbed a thick handful of Preston's hair, yanked hard, and wrenched out from under the weight on his chest. Like a cat he was up. But

Preston stepped on one foot and kicked the other out from under him, the tactic he had apparently used when Duncan had the snake in his arms.

In the flash of time it took to spring back to his feet, Duncan caught on to a new course. Strategies he had learned from Perry came back to him, things a small man in combat with a big one ought to know, like the importance of surprise and balance. He lunged in, caught Preston by the arm, darted back and tripped him over his leg. Preston came up yelling. He swung at Duncan with his fist, but Duncan kicked up his elbow and the blow skimmed wide, while the punch Duncan sent to Preston's stomach landed full force. Duncan tackled while Preston was doubled over.

Over and over they rolled in the dirt. To stay in motion, to not get pinned, was what mattered. It seemed that Preston became more and more clumsy while Duncan's command of himself hummed along like a warm motor.

But now, the stars were spinning around again. His eyes were closed, his mouth open, full of dust and the taste of blood that ran down from a cut on his eyebrow. Clutched in his hands was one of Preston's feet. He twisted it around and around as Preston, trying to get loose, kicked at him with the other foot and slowly crawled through the dirt, dragging him over a stick of firewood that cut into the skin left bare by the split in his fringed loincloth. One thing to do . . . hold on, hold on, hold on.

Then abruptly the pulling stopped and the foot was loose in his hands. He didn't open his eyes, but he knew it was Don's hand on his shoulder, Don on the ground beside him, saying, "Duncan, Duncan, let go."

There was something in Don's voice that ended the fight. He let go of the hated foot and let himself be gathered into Don's arms. Although he gasped for breath, inside he was calm and satisfied. His whole body ached, yet he was happy. And he knew Don understood.

He knew by the gentleness in Don's command, ". . . let go," and by the way he sat quietly on the ground and stroked Duncan's wet hair back off his forehead. Don was glad of the fight and the way it ended with Preston crawling away. Don's cheek, like his jacket, was smeared with blood and the colors of war paint. He smiled at Duncan, his good Abe Lincoln smile, and said, "That was some fight, my friend."

The solemn gladness swelled inside, so ripe that Duncan wanted to cry for relief. But, of course, he couldn't cry. Boys didn't, if they could help it, and *he*, though he was bruised and exhausted, could help it.

He could also stand on his feet, which he did,
supported by Don. On legs as weak as rope, he
walked to the bench, where he almost fell as he bent
his knees to sit down. Don caught him with an arm
around his shoulders.

The campers stood in a half circle, openmouthed
and frozen, as they had been before the living snake.
Uncle Murdock, in a husky voice, told them good
night. Obediently, in slow motion, they turned to
the lighted path. Only the boys of Bear Cabin
remained.

Tully pulled off his shirt. "He's bleeding, Don."
Gently Don wiped Duncan's face on Tully's shirt.
Frank and Sid watched, unmoving. Pete, Joe, and
Jeep kneeled in the dust at Don's feet.

"You really *got* Preston," Joe said softly, beginning to bounce on his heels.

"He sure as heck did," Frank said, coming out of his trance. He sighed and passed his fingers through his thick dark curls.

Sid nodded, his cracked tooth suddenly gleaming in a quick smile. "He had it coming! He's been a pain in the neck ever since baseball."

Pete looked down at the tracks he was drawing in the dust. "It was great, Duncan, really great."

"Frank, go check on Preston, would you?" Don said.

"Let him fend for himself," Frank said with a snort. "I hope he's got a fat lip."

Uncle Murdock came up, panting heavily, and said that Dr. Madison was checking Preston at the infirmary. "I've already spoken to the boy," he said to Don, "so you won't have to. He'll sleep at the infirmary tonight."

"That was a lousy thing he did, Uncle Murdock," Frank said. "You just got through promising you wouldn't let anybody kill that snake. *Anybody* could see it was tame."

"Where is the snake?" Duncan asked.

"Don't look at it, Dunc." Jeep shook his head, frowning.

"That's okay, Jeep. I've seen dead snakes before."

"But it's not dead yet."

Sid and Frank moved aside, and they all looked back at the snake, turning over and over slowly in front of the dying Council Fire. "Yes, it's dead," Duncan said. "They always move a long time after."

Dr. Madison paused to look at the snake, as he came across the Council Ring. "You're quite a snake handler, young man," he said, sitting down on the bench beside Duncan. "Let's see what we can find wrong here."

Uncle Murdock, strangely subdued, stood watching the examination, wavering slightly from side to side, his big moccasined feet planted wide apart, one hand hanging loose at his side, the other pulling at his chin, making the dent deeper.

Dr. Madison stood up when he had looked Duncan over carefully. He folded up his black-rimmed glasses and put them in a case. Duncan had no broken bones, he assured Uncle Murdock, only some places that needed cleaning up, a small cut on his eyebrow, and several abrasions on the skin of the back and sides with retained particles of sand and grit. He turned to Don. "Don, I want you to carry this boy back to the cabin. He's had enough exercise for today." He told Duncan to take a shower with antiseptic soap and he would be over to finish the clean-up and put on the bandages.

Duncan was glad of the ride to the cabin on Don's back. He felt as weak as Jello. He jogged along, his head on Don's shoulder, hardly able to keep his eyes open. Jeep held the screen door. The first-aid kit lay open on Don's bed. Everyone watched silently as Frank took the wrapper off a new bar of antiseptic soap.

The lights were out now and Duncan lay between the sheets feeling the clean smart of his injuries. He listened to the wind sighing in the tops of the trees. A pine cone dropped on the roof and staggered over the shingles to thump into a soft bed of needles.

On the porch, Uncle Murdock, Don, and the doctor talked in low voices. Then the spring on the screen door strained and Uncle Murdock came in. He filled the whole doorway. His flashlight beamed on the floor as he bent down in the narrow aisle between Duncan's bed and Sid's. "You feeling all right, Duncan?"

"I'm fine, Uncle Murdock."

"Duncan, I want to say to you before you go to sleep that I'm sorry I didn't understand about your king snake so you could have felt free to confide in me. I'm sorry for what happened. We'll be careful not to kill any king snakes or other harmless snakes after this."

"Really, Uncle Murdock?"

"Yes, Duncan. You've shown me that an old man is not necessarily wise in matters that touch the heart. But let us not believe that an old dog cannot learn."

"You could import some king snakes, Uncle Murdock, and then you wouldn't have to worry about the poisonous kind. I know a catalog where you could order some. But they're expensive. Five dollars apiece."

"That's not too much to pay for a watch dog, Duncan. You give me that address and if the native ones don't come back, we shall import some."

The adhesive tape over Duncan's temple wrinkled and pulled, but he smiled anyway. "That's good, Uncle Murdock."

Uncle Murdock squeezed Duncan's shoulder and heaved his great bulk up. When he was gone, the bed springs all gently creaked and Duncan knew that everyone who had been listening now sank his head into the pillow.

ABOUT THE AUTHOR

A graduate of Wheaton College in Norton, Massachusetts, Helen Copeland was born in Rochester, Minnesota. She did graduate study at Brown University in the field of zoology and studied creative writing at Queen's Evening College in Charlotte, North Carolina, where she now lives with her four children. Articles and short stories by Mrs. Copeland have appeared in *Redbook* and *Cosmopolitan*.

The main character of *This Snake Is Good*, Duncan McKenna, is a composite of the author's three sons. He is also the hero of *Duncan's World*, another of Mrs. Copeland's books for children.

ABOUT THE ILLUSTRATOR

A recipient of the Western Writers of America Cover Art Award, Charles W. Walker has provided illustrations for many children's books and for several magazines, including *Harper's*, *Horizon*, and *Good Housekeeping*.

Mr. Walker was graduated *cum laude* from Syracuse University, after which he traveled extensively in Europe, sketching and painting. He attended the Art Students League in New York City and studied with John Groth and Joseph Hirsch. He lives in Roosevelt, New York, with his wife and six children.